Probl

Agatha of Crime. Her books have sold over a billion copies in English with another billion in 100 foreign countries. She is the most widely published author of all time and in any language, outsold only by the Bible and Shakespeare. She is the author of 80 crime novels and short story collections, 19 plays, and six novels written under the name of Mary Westmacott.

Agatha Christie's first novel, *The Mysterious Affair at Styles*, was written towards the end of the First World War, in which she served as a VAD. In it she created Hercule Poirot, the little Belgian detective who was destined to become the most popular detective in crime fiction since Sherlock Holmes. It was eventually published by The Bodley Head in 1920.

In 1926, after averaging a book a year, Agatha Christie wrote her masterpiece. *The Murder of Roger Ackroyd* was the first of her books to be published by Collins and marked the beginning of an author-publisher relationship which lasted for 50 years and well over 70 books. *The Murder of Roger Ackroyd* was also the first of Agatha Christie's books to be dramatised – under the name *Alibi* – and to have a successful run in London's West End. *The Mousetrap*, her most famous play of all, opened in 1952 and is the longest-running play in history.

Agatha Christie was made a Dame in 1971. She died in 1976, since when a number of books have been published posthumously: the bestselling novel *Sleeping Murder* appeared later that year, followed by her autobiography and the short story collections *Miss Marple's Final Cases*, *Problem at Pollensa Bay* and *While the Light Lasts*. In 1998 *Black Coffee* was the first of her plays to be novelized by another author, Charles Osborne.

The Agatha Christie Collection

The Man In The Brown Suit
The Secret of Chimneys
The Seven Dials Mystery
The Mysterious Mr Quin
The Sittaford Mystery
The Hound of Death
The Listerdale Mystery
Why Didn't They Ask Evans?
Parker Pyne Investigates
Murder Is Easy
And Then There Were None
Towards Zero
Death Comes as the End
Sparkling Cyanide
Crooked House
They Came to Baghdad
Destination Unknown
Spider's Web *
The Unexpected Guest *
Ordeal by Innocence
The Pale Horse
Endless Night
Passenger To Frankfurt
Problem at Pollensa Bay
While the Light Lasts

Poirot

The Mysterious Affair at Styles
The Murder on the Links
Poirot Investigates
The Murder of Roger Ackroyd
The Big Four
The Mystery of the Blue Train
Black Coffee *
Peril at End House
Lord Edgware Dies
Murder on the Orient Express
Three-Act Tragedy
Death in the Clouds
The ABC Murders
Murder in Mesopotamia
Cards on the Table
Murder in the Mews
Dumb Witness
Death on the Nile
Appointment With Death
Hercule Poirot's Christmas
Sad Cypress
One, Two, Buckle My Shoe
Evil Under the Sun
Five Little Pigs
The Hollow
The Labours of Hercules
Taken at the Flood
Mrs McGinty's Dead
After the Funeral
Hickory Dickory Dock
Dead Man's Folly
Cat Among the Pigeons
The Adventure of the Christmas Pudding
The Clocks
Third Girl
Hallowe'en Party
Elephants Can Remember
Poirot's Early Cases
Curtain: Poirot's Last Case

Marple

The Murder at the Vicarage
The Thirteen Problems
The Body in the Library
The Moving Finger
A Murder is Announced
They Do It With Mirrors
A Pocket Full of Rye
The 4.50 from Paddington
The Mirror Crack'd from Side to Side
A Caribbean Mystery
At Bertram's Hotel
Nemesis
Sleeping Murder
Miss Marple's Final Cases

Tommy & Tuppence

The Secret Adversary
Partners in Crime
N or M?
By the Pricking of My Thumbs
Postern of Fate

Published as Mary Westmacott

Giant's Bread
Unfinished Portrait
Absent in the Spring
The Rose and the Yew Tree
A Daughter's a Daughter
The Burden

Memoirs

An Autobiography
Come, Tell Me How You Live

Play Collections

The Mousetrap and Selected Plays
Witness for the Prosecution and Selected Plays

* novelised by Charles Osborne

Agatha Christie

Problem at Pollensa Bay

HARPER

HARPER

An imprint of HarperCollins*Publishers*
77–85 Fulham Palace Road
Hammersmith, London W6 8JB
www.harpercollins.co.uk

This *Agatha Christie Signature Edition* published 2003
2 4 6 8 10 9 7 5 3

First published in Great Britain by
HarperCollins*Publishers* 1991

ISBN 978-0-00-729956-0

Typeset by Palimpsest Book Production Limited,
Grangemouth, Stirlingshire

Printed and bound in India by
Gopsons Papers Ltd., Noida

Contents

Problem at Pollensa Bay

I

The steamer from Barcelona to Majorca landed Mr Parker Pyne at Palma in the early hours of the morning – and straightaway he met with disillusionment. The hotels were full! The best that could be done for him was an airless cupboard overlooking an inner court in a hotel in the centre of the town – and with that Mr Parker Pyne was not prepared to put up. The proprietor of the hotel was indifferent to his disappointment.

'What will you?' he observed with a shrug.

Palma was popular now! The exchange was favourable! Everyone – the English, the Americans – they all came to Majorca in the winter. The whole place was crowded. It was doubtful if the English gentleman would be able to get in anywhere – except perhaps at Formentor where the prices were so ruinous that even foreigners blenched at them.

Mr Parker Pyne partook of some coffee and a roll

and went out to view the cathedral, but found himself in no mood for appreciating the beauties of architecture.

He next had a conference with a friendly taxi driver in inadequate French interlarded with native Spanish, and they discussed the merits and possibilities of Soller, Alcudia, Pollensa and Formentor – where there were fine hotels but very expensive.

Mr Parker Pyne was goaded to inquire how expensive.

They asked, said the taxi driver, an amount that it would be absurd and ridiculous to pay – was it not well known that the English came here because prices were cheap and reasonable?

Mr Parker Pyne said that that was quite so, but all the same what sums *did* they charge at Formentor?

A price incredible!

Perfectly – but WHAT PRICE EXACTLY?

The driver consented at last to reply in terms of figures.

Fresh from the exactions of hotels in Jerusalem and Egypt, the figure did not stagger Mr Parker Pyne unduly.

A bargain was struck, Mr Parker Pyne's suitcases were loaded on the taxi in a somewhat haphazard manner, and they started off to drive round the island, trying cheaper hostelries en route but with the final objective of Formentor.

But they never reached that final abode of plutocracy, for after they had passed through the narrow streets of Pollensa and were following the curved line of the seashore, they came to the Hotel Pino d'Oro – a small hotel standing on the edge of the sea looking out over a view that in the misty haze of a fine morning had the exquisite vagueness of a Japanese print. At once Mr Parker Pyne knew that this, and this only, was what he was looking for. He stopped the taxi, passed through the painted gate with the hope that he would find a resting place.

The elderly couple to whom the hotel belonged knew no English or French. Nevertheless the matter was concluded satisfactorily. Mr Parker Pyne was allotted a room overlooking the sea, the suitcases were unloaded, the driver congratulated his passenger upon avoiding the monstrous exigencies of 'these new hotels', received his fare and departed with a cheerful Spanish salutation.

Mr Parker Pyne glanced at his watch and perceiving that it was, even now, but a quarter to ten, he went out onto the small terrace now bathed in a dazzling morning light and ordered, for the second time that morning, coffee and rolls.

There were four tables there, his own, one from which breakfast was being cleared away and two occupied ones. At the one nearest him sat a family of father and mother and two elderly daughters – Germans. Beyond them, at the corner of the terrace, sat what were clearly an English mother and son.

The woman was about fifty-five. She had grey hair of a pretty tone – was sensibly but not fashionably dressed in a tweed coat and skirt – and had that comfortable self-possession which marks an Englishwoman used to much travelling abroad.

The young man who sat opposite her might have been twenty-five and he too was typical of his class and age. He was neither good-looking nor plain, tall nor short. He was clearly on the best of terms with his mother – they made little jokes together – and he was assiduous in passing her things.

As they talked, her eye met that of Mr Parker Pyne. It passed over him with well-bred nonchalance, but he knew that he had been assimilated and labelled.

He had been recognized as English and doubtless, in due course, some pleasant non-committal remark would be addressed to him.

Mr Parker Pyne had no particular objection. His own countrymen and women abroad were inclined to bore him slightly, but he was quite willing to pass the time of day in an amiable manner. In a small hotel it caused constraint if one did not do so. This particular woman, he felt sure, had excellent 'hotel manners', as he put it.

The English boy rose from his seat, made some

laughing remark and passed into the hotel. The woman took her letters and bag and settled herself in a chair facing the sea. She unfolded a copy of the *Continental Daily Mail.* Her back was to Mr Parker Pyne.

As he drank the last drop of his coffee, Mr Parker Pyne glanced in her direction, and instantly he stiffened. He was alarmed – alarmed for the peaceful continuance of his holiday! That back was horribly expressive. In his time he had classified many such backs. Its rigidity – the tenseness of its poise – without seeing her face he knew well enough that the eyes were bright with unshed tears – that the woman was keeping herself in hand by a rigid effort.

Moving warily, like a much-hunted animal, Mr Parker Pyne retreated into the hotel. Not half an hour before he had been invited to sign his name in the book lying on the desk. There it was – a neat signature – C. Parker Pyne, London.

A few lines above Mr Parker Pyne noticed the entries: Mrs R. Chester, Mr Basil Chester – Holm Park, Devon.

Seizing a pen, Mr Parker Pyne wrote rapidly over his signature. It now read (with difficulty) Christopher Pyne.

If Mrs R. Chester was unhappy in Pollensa Bay, it was not going to be made easy for her to consult Mr Parker Pyne.

Already it had been a source of abiding wonder to that gentleman that so many people he had come across abroad should know his name and have noted his advertisements. In England many thousands of people read the *Times* every day and could have answered quite truthfully that they had never heard such a name in their lives. Abroad, he reflected, they read their newspapers more thoroughly. No item, not even the advertisement columns, escaped them.

Already his holidays had been interrupted on several occasions. He had dealt with a whole series of problems from murder to attempted blackmail. He was determined in Majorca to have peace. He felt instinctively that a distressed mother might trouble that peace considerably.

Mr Parker Pyne settled down at the Pino d'Oro very happily. There was a larger hotel not far off, the Mariposa, where a good many English people stayed. There was also quite an artist colony living all round. You could walk along by the sea to the fishing village where there was a cocktail bar where people met – there were a few shops. It was all very peaceful and pleasant. Girls strolled about in trousers with brightly coloured handkerchiefs tied round the upper halves of their bodies. Young men in berets with rather long hair held forth in 'Mac's Bar' on such subjects as plastic values and abstraction in art.

On the day after Mr Parker Pyne's arrival, Mrs Chester made a few conventional remarks to him on the subject of the view and the likelihood of the weather keeping fine. She then chatted a little with the German lady about knitting, and had a few pleasant words about the sadness of the political situation with two Danish gentlemen who spent their time rising at dawn and walking for eleven hours.

Mr Parker Pyne found Basil Chester a most likeable young man. He called Mr Parker Pyne 'sir' and listened most politely to anything the older man said. Sometimes the three English people had coffee together after dinner in the evening. After the third day, Basil left the party after ten minutes or so and Mr Parker Pyne was left tête-à-tête with Mrs Chester.

They talked about flowers and the growing of them, of the lamentable state of the English pound and of how expensive France had become, and of the difficulty of getting good afternoon tea.

Every evening when her son departed, Mr Parker Pyne saw the quickly concealed tremor of her lips, but immediately she recovered and discoursed pleasantly on the above-mentioned subjects.

Little by little she began to talk of Basil – of how well he had done at school – 'he was in the First XI, you know' – of how everyone liked him, of how proud his father would have been of the boy had he lived, of how thankful she had been that Basil had never been 'wild'. 'Of course I always urge him to be with young people, but he really seems to prefer being with me.'

She said it with a kind of nice modest pleasure in the fact.

But for once Mr Parker Pyne did not make the usual tactful response he could usually achieve so easily. He said instead:

'Oh! well, there seem to be plenty of young people here – not in the hotel, but round about.'

At that, he noticed, Mrs Chester stiffened. She said: Of course there were a lot of *artists*. Perhaps she was very old-fashioned – *real* art, of course, was different, but a lot of young people just made that sort of thing an excuse for lounging about and doing nothing – and the girls drank a lot too much.

On the following day Basil said to Mr Parker Pyne:

'I'm awfully glad you turned up here, sir – especially for my mother's sake. She likes having you to talk to in the evenings.'

'What did you do when you were first here?'

'As a matter of fact we used to play piquet.'

'I see.'

'Of course one gets rather tired of piquet. As a matter of fact I've got some friends here – frightfully cheery crowd. I don't really think my mother approves of them –' He laughed as though he felt this ought to be amusing. 'The mater's very old-fashioned . . . Even girls in trousers shock her!'

'Quite so,' said Mr Parker Pyne.

'What I tell her is – one's got to move with the times . . . The girls at home round us are frightfully dull . . .'

'I see,' said Mr Parker Pyne.

All this interested him well enough. He was a spectator of a miniature drama, but he was not called upon to take part in it.

And then the worst – from Mr Parker Pyne's point of view – happened. A gushing lady of his acquaintance came to stay at the Mariposa. They met in the tea shop in the presence of Mrs Chester.

The newcomer screamed:

'Why – if it isn't Mr Parker Pyne – the one and only Mr Parker Pyne! And Adela Chester! Do you know each other? Oh, you do? You're staying at the same hotel? He's the one and only original wizard, Adela – the marvel of the century – all your troubles smoothed out while you wait! Didn't you *know*? You must have *heard* about him? Haven't you read his advertisements? "*Are you in trouble? Consult Mr Parker Pyne.*" There's just nothing he can't do. Husbands and wives flying at each other's throats and he brings 'em together – if you've lost interest in life he gives you the most thrilling adventures. As I say the man's just a *wizard*!'

It went on a good deal longer – Mr Parker Pyne at intervals making modest disclaimers. He disliked the look that Mrs Chester turned upon him. He disliked even more seeing her return along the beach in close confabulation with the garrulous singer of his praises.

The climax came quicker than he expected. That evening, after coffee, Mrs Chester said abruptly,

'Will you come into the little salon, Mr Pyne? There is something I want to say to you.'

He could but bow and submit.

Mrs Chester's self-control had been wearing thin – as the door of the little salon closed behind them, it snapped. She sat down and burst into tears.

'My boy, Mr Parker Pyne. You must save him. *We* must save him. It's breaking my heart!'

'My dear lady, as a mere outsider –'

'Nina Wycherley says you can do *anything*. She said I was to have the utmost confidence in you. She advised me to tell you everything – and that you'd put the whole thing right.'

Inwardly Mr Parker Pyne cursed the obtrusive Mrs Wycherley.

Resigning himself he said:

'Well, let us thrash the matter out. A girl, I suppose?'

'Did he tell you about her?'

'Only indirectly.'

Words poured in a vehement stream from Mrs Chester. 'The girl was dreadful. She drank, she swore – she wore no clothes to speak of. Her sister lived out here – was married to an artist – a Dutchman. The whole set was most undesirable. Half of them were living together without being married. Basil was completely changed. He had always been so quiet, so interested in serious subjects. He had thought at one time of taking up archaeology –'

'Well, well,' said Mr Parker Pyne. 'Nature will have her revenge.'

'What do you mean?'

'It isn't healthy for a young man to be interested in serious subjects. He ought to be making an idiot of himself over one girl after another.'

'Please be serious, Mr Pyne.'

'I'm perfectly serious. Is the young lady, by any chance, the one who had tea with you yesterday?'

He had noticed her – her grey flannel trousers – the scarlet handkerchief tied loosely around her breast – the vermilion mouth and the fact that she had chosen a cocktail in preference to tea.

'You saw her? Terrible! Not the kind of girl Basil has ever admired.'

'You haven't given him much chance to admire a girl, have you?'

'I?'

'He's been too fond of *your* company! Bad! However, I daresay he'll get over this – if you don't precipitate matters.'

'You don't understand. He wants to marry this girl – Betty Gregg – they're *engaged*.'

'It's gone as far as that?'

'Yes. Mr Parker Pyne, you *must* do something. You must get my boy out of this disastrous marriage! His whole life will be ruined.'

'Nobody's life can be ruined except by themselves.'

'Basil's will be,' said Mrs Chester positively.

'I'm not worrying about Basil.'

'You're not worrying about the *girl*?'

'No, I'm worrying about *you*. You've been squandering your birthright.'

Mrs Chester looked at him, slightly taken aback.

'What are the years from twenty to forty? Fettered and bound by personal and emotional relationships. That's bound to be. That's living. But later there's a new stage. You can think, observe life, discover something about other people and the truth about yourself. Life becomes real – significant. You see it as a whole. Not just one scene – the scene you, as an actor, are playing. No man or woman is actually himself (or herself) till after forty-five. That's when individuality has a chance.'

Mrs Chester said:

'I've been wrapped up in Basil. He's been *everything* to me.'

'Well, he shouldn't have been. That's what you're paying for now. Love him as much as you like – but you're Adela Chester, remember, a person – not just Basil's mother.'

'It will break my heart if Basil's life is ruined,' said Basil's mother.

He looked at the delicate lines of her face, the wistful droop of her mouth. She was, somehow, a lovable woman. He did not want her to be hurt. He said:

'I'll see what I can do.'

He found Basil Chester only too ready to talk, eager to urge his point of view.

'This business is being just hellish. Mother's hopeless – prejudiced, narrow-minded. If only she'd let herself, she'd *see* how fine Betty is.'

'And Betty?'

He sighed.

'Betty's being damned difficult! If she'd just conform a bit – I mean leave off the lipstick for a day – it might make all the difference. She seems to go out of her way to be – well – modern – when Mother's about.'

Mr Parker Pyne smiled.

'Betty and Mother are two of the dearest people in the world, I should have thought they would have taken to each other like hot cakes.'

'You have a lot to learn, young man,' said Mr Parker Pyne.

'I wish you'd come along and see Betty and have a good talk about it all.'

Mr Parker Pyne accepted the invitation readily.

Betty and her sister and her husband lived in a small dilapidated villa a little way back from the sea. Their life was of a refreshing simplicity. Their furniture comprised three chairs, a table and beds. There was a cupboard in the wall that held the bare requirements of cups and plates. Hans was an excitable young man with wild blond hair that stood up all over his head. He spoke very odd English with incredible rapidity, walking up and down as he did so. Stella, his wife, was small and fair. Betty Gregg had red hair and freckles and a mischievous eye. She was, he noticed, not nearly so made-up as she had been the previous day at the Pino d'Oro.

She gave him a cocktail and said with a twinkle:

'You're in on the big bust-up?'

Mr Parker Pyne nodded.

'And whose side are you on, big boy? The young lovers – or the disapproving dame?'

'May I ask you a question?'

'Certainly.'

'Have you been very tactful over all this?'

'Not at all,' said Miss Gregg frankly. 'But the old cat

put my back up.' (She glanced round to make sure that Basil was out of earshot) 'That woman just makes me feel mad. She's kept Basil tied to her apron strings all these years – that sort of thing makes a man look a fool. Basil isn't a fool really. Then she's so terribly *pukka sahib*.'

'That's not really such a bad thing. It's merely "unfashionable" just at present.'

Betty Gregg gave a sudden twinkle.

'You mean it's like putting Chippendale chairs in the attic in Victorian days? Later you get them down again and say, "Aren't they marvellous?"'

'Something of the kind.'

Betty Gregg considered.

'Perhaps you're right. I'll be honest. It was Basil who put my back up – being so anxious about what impression I'd make on his mother. It drove me to extremes. Even now I believe he might give me up – if his mother worked on him good and hard.'

'He might,' said Mr Parker Pyne. 'If she went about it the right way.'

'Are you going to tell her the right way? She won't think of it herself, you know. She'll just go on disapproving and that won't do the trick. But if you prompted her –'

She bit her lip – raised frank blue eyes to his.

'I've heard about you, Mr Parker Pyne. You're supposed to know something about human nature.

Do you think Basil and I could make a go of it – or not?'

'I should like an answer to three questions.'

'Suitability test? All right, go ahead.'

'Do you sleep with your window open or shut?'

'Open. I like lots of air.'

'Do you and Basil enjoy the same kind of food?'

'Yes.'

'Do you like going to bed early or late?'

'Really, under the rose, early. At half past ten I yawn – and I secretly feel rather hearty in the mornings – but of course I daren't admit it.'

'You ought to suit each other very well,' said Mr Parker Pyne.

'Rather a superficial test.'

'Not at all. I have known seven marriages at least, entirely wrecked, because the husband liked sitting up till midnight and the wife fell asleep at half past nine and vice versa.'

'It's a pity,' said Betty, 'that everybody can't be happy. Basil and I, and his mother giving us her blessing.'

Mr Parker Pyne coughed.

'I think,' he said, 'that that could possibly be managed.'

She looked at him doubtfully.

'Now I wonder,' she said, 'if you're double-crossing me?'

Mr Parker Pyne's face told nothing.

To Mrs Chester he was soothing, but vague. An engagement was not marriage. He himself was going to Soller for a week. He suggested that her line of action should be non-committal. Let her appear to acquiesce.

He spent a very enjoyable week at Soller.

On his return he found that a totally unexpected development had arisen.

As he entered the Pino d'Oro the first thing he saw was Mrs Chester and Betty Gregg having tea together. Basil was not there. Mrs Chester looked haggard. Betty, too, was looking off colour. She was hardly made-up at all, and her eyelids looked as though she had been crying.

They greeted him in a friendly fashion, but neither of them mentioned Basil.

Suddenly he heard the girl beside him draw in her breath sharply as though something had hurt her. Mr Parker Pyne turned his head.

Basil Chester was coming up the steps from the sea front. With him was a girl so exotically beautiful that it quite took your breath away. She was dark and her figure was marvellous. No one could fail to notice the fact since she wore nothing but a single garment of pale blue crêpe. She was heavily made-up with ochre powder and an orange scarlet mouth – but the unguents only displayed her remarkable beauty in a more pronounced fashion. As for young Basil, he seemed unable to take his eyes from her face.

'You're very late, Basil,' said his mother. 'You were to have taken Betty to Mac's.'

'My fault,' drawled the beautiful unknown. 'We just drifted.' She turned to Basil. 'Angel – get me something with a kick in it!'

She tossed off her shoe and stretched out her manicured toenails which were done emerald green to match her fingernails.

She paid no attention to the two women, but she leaned a little towards Mr Parker Pyne.

'Terrible island this,' she said. 'I was just dying with boredom before I met Basil. He *is* rather a pet!'

'Mr Parker Pyne – Miss Ramona,' said Mrs Chester.

The girl acknowledged the introduction with a lazy smile.

'I guess I'll call you Parker almost at once,' she murmured. 'My name's Dolores.'

Basil returned with the drinks. Miss Ramona divided her conversation (what there was of it – it was mostly glances) between Basil and Mr Parker Pyne. Of the two women she took no notice whatever. Betty attempted once or twice to join in the conversation but the other girl merely stared at her and yawned.

Suddenly Dolores rose.

'Guess I'll be going along now. I'm at the other hotel. Anyone coming to see me home?'

Basil sprang up.

'I'll come with you.'

Mrs Chester said: 'Basil, my dear –'

'I'll be back presently, Mother.'

'Isn't he the mother's boy?' Miss Ramona asked of the world at large. 'Just toots round after her, don't you?'

Basil flushed and looked awkward. Miss Ramona gave a nod in Mrs Chester's direction, a dazzling smile to Mr Parker Pyne and she and Basil moved off together.

After they had gone there was rather an awkward silence. Mr Parker Pyne did not like to speak first. Betty Gregg was twisting her fingers and looking out to sea. Mrs Chester looked flushed and angry.

Betty said: 'Well, what do you think of our new acquisition in Pollensa Bay?' Her voice was not quite steady.

Mr Parker Pyne said cautiously:

'A little – er – exotic.'

'Exotic?' Betty gave a short bitter laugh.

Mrs Chester said: 'She's terrible – terrible. Basil must be quite mad.'

Betty said sharply: 'Basil's all right.'

'Her toenails,' said Mrs Chester with a shiver of nausea.

Betty rose suddenly.

'I think, Mrs Chester, I'll go home and not stay to dinner after all.'

'Oh, my dear – Basil will be so disappointed.'

'Will he?' asked Betty with a short laugh. 'Anyway, I think I will. I've got rather a headache.'

She smiled at them both and went off. Mrs Chester turned to Mr Parker Pyne.

'I wish we had never come to this place – never!'

Mr Parker Pyne shook his head sadly.

'You shouldn't have gone away,' said Mrs Chester. 'If you'd been here this wouldn't have happened.'

Mr Parker Pyne was stung to respond.

'My dear lady, I can assure you that when it comes to a question of a beautiful young woman, I should have no influence over your son whatever. He – er – seems to be of a very susceptible nature.'

'He never used to be,' said Mrs Chester tearfully.

'Well,' said Mr Parker Pyne with an attempt at cheerfulness, 'this new attraction seems to have broken the back of his infatuation for Miss Gregg. That must be some satisfaction to you.'

'I don't know what you mean,' said Mrs Chester. 'Betty is a dear child and devoted to Basil. She is behaving extremely well over this. I think my boy must be mad.'

Mr Parker Pyne received this startling change of face

without wincing. He had met inconsistency in women before. He said mildly:

'Not exactly mad – just bewitched.'

'The creature's a Dago. She's impossible.'

'But extremely good-looking.'

Mrs Chester snorted.

Basil ran up the steps from the sea front.

'Hullo, Mater, here I am. Where's Betty?'

'Betty's gone home with a headache. I don't wonder.'

'Sulking, you mean.'

'I consider, Basil, that you are being extremely unkind to Betty.'

'For God's sake, Mother, don't jaw. If Betty is going to make this fuss every time I speak to another girl a nice sort of life we'll lead together.'

'You *are* engaged.'

'Oh, we're engaged all right. That doesn't mean that we're not going to have any friends of our own. Nowadays people have to lead their own lives and try to cut out jealousy.'

He paused.

'Look here, if Betty isn't going to dine with us – I think I'll go back to the Mariposa. They did ask me to dine . . .'

'Oh, Basil –'

The boy gave her an exasperated look, then ran off down the steps.

Mrs Chester looked eloquently at Mr Parker Pyne. 'You see,' she said.

He saw.

Matters came to a head a couple of days later. Betty and Basil were to have gone for a long walk, taking a picnic lunch with them. Betty arrived at the Pino d'Oro to find that Basil had forgotten the plan and gone over to Formentor for the day with Dolores Ramona's party.

Beyond a tightening of the lips the girl made no sign. Presently, however, she got up and stood in front of Mrs Chester (the two women were alone on the terrace).

'It's quite all right,' she said. 'It doesn't matter. But I think – all the same – that we'd better call the whole thing off.'

She slipped from her finger the signet ring that Basil had given her – he would buy the real engagement ring later.

'Will you give him back this Mrs Chester? And tell him it's all right – not to worry . . .'

'Betty dear, don't! He *does* love you – really.'

'It looks like it, doesn't it?' said the girl with a short laugh. 'No – I've got some pride. Tell him everything's all right and that I – I wish him luck.'

When Basil returned at sunset he was greeted by a storm.

He flushed a little at the sight of his ring.

'So that's how she feels, is it? Well, I daresay it's the best thing.'

'Basil!'

'Well, frankly, Mother, we don't seem to have been hitting it off lately.'

'Whose fault was that?'

'I don't see that it was mine particularly. Jealousy's beastly and I really don't see why *you* should get all worked up about it. You begged me yourself not to marry Betty.'

'That was before I knew her. Basil – my dear – you're not thinking of marrying this other creature.'

Basil Chester said soberly:

'I'd marry her like a shot if she'd have me – but I'm afraid she won't.'

Cold chills went down Mrs Chester's spine. She sought and found Mr Parker Pyne, placidly reading a book in a sheltered corner.

'You must *do* something! You *must* do something! My boy's life will be ruined.'

Mr Parker Pyne was getting a little tired of Basil Chester's life being ruined.

'What can I do?'

'Go and see this terrible creature. If necessary buy her off.'

'That may come very expensive.'

'I don't care.'

'It seems a pity. Still there are, possibly, other ways.'

She looked a question. He shook his head.

'I'll make no promises – but I'll see what I can do. I have handled that kind before. By the way, not a word to Basil – that would be fatal.'

'Of course not.'

Mr Parker Pyne returned from the Mariposa at midnight. Mrs Chester was sitting up for him.

'Well?' she demanded breathlessly.

His eyes twinkled.

'The Señorita Dolores Ramona will leave Pollensa tomorrow morning and the island tomorrow night.'

'Oh, Mr Parker Pyne! How did you manage it?'

'It won't cost a cent,' said Mr Parker Pyne. Again his eyes twinkled. 'I rather fancied I might have a hold over her – and I was right.'

'You are wonderful. Nina Wycherley was quite right. You must let me know – er – your fees –'

Mr Parker Pyne held up a well-manicured hand.

'Not a penny. It has been a pleasure. I hope all will go well. Of course the boy will be very upset at first when he finds she's disappeared and left no address. Just go easy with him for a week or two.'

'If only Betty will forgive him –'

'She'll forgive him all right. They're a nice couple. By the way, I'm leaving tomorrow, too.'

'Oh, Mr Parker Pyne, we shall miss you.'

'Perhaps it's just as well I should go before that boy of yours gets infatuated with yet a third girl.'

II

Mr Parker Pyne leaned over the rail of the steamer and looked at the lights of Palma. Beside him stood Dolores Ramona. He was saying appreciatively:

'A very nice piece of work, Madeleine. I'm glad I wired you to come out. It's odd when you're such a quiet, stay-at-home girl really.'

Madeleine de Sara, alias Dolores Ramona, alias Maggie Sayers, said primly: 'I'm glad you're pleased, Mr Parker Pyne. It's been a nice little change. I think I'll go below now and get to bed before the boat starts. I'm such a bad sailor.'

A few minutes later a hand fell on Mr Parker Pyne's shoulder. He turned to see Basil Chester.

'Had to come and see you off, Mr Parker Pyne, and give you Betty's love and her and my best thanks. It was a grand stunt of yours. Betty and Mother are as thick as thieves. Seemed a shame to deceive the old darling – but she *was* being difficult. Anyway it's all right now. I must just be careful to keep up the annoyance stuff a couple of days longer. We're no end grateful to you, Betty and I.'

'I wish you every happiness,' said Mr Parker Pyne.

'Thanks.'

There was a pause, then Basil said with somewhat overdone carelessness:

'Is Miss – Miss de Sara – anywhere about? I'd like to thank her, too.'

Mr Parker Pyne shot a keen glance at him.

He said:

'I'm afraid Miss de Sara's gone to bed.'

'Oh, too bad – well, perhaps I'll see her in London sometime.'

'As a matter of fact she is going to America on business for me almost at once.'

'Oh!' Basil's tone was blank. 'Well,' he said. 'I'll be getting along . . .'

Mr Parker Pyne smiled. On his way to his cabin he tapped on the door of Madeleine's.

'How are you, my dear? All right? Our young friend has been along. The usual slight attack of Madeleinitis. He'll get over it in a day or two, but you are rather distracting.'

The Second Gong

Joan Ashby came out of her bedroom and stood a moment on the landing outside her door. She was half turning as if to go back into the room when, below her feet as it seemed, a gong boomed out.

Immediately Joan started forward almost at a run. So great was her hurry that at the top of the big staircase she collided with a young man arriving from the opposite direction.

'Hullo, Joan! Why the wild hurry?'

'Sorry, Harry. I didn't see you.'

'So I gathered,' said Harry Dalehouse dryly. 'But as I say, why the wild haste?'

'It was the gong.'

'I know. But it's only the first gong.'

'No, it's the second.'

'First.'

'Second.'

Thus arguing they had been descending the stairs. They were now in the hall, where the butler, having replaced the gongstick, was advancing toward them at a grave and dignified pace.

'It is the second,' persisted Joan. 'I know it is. Well, for one thing, look at the time.'

Harry Dalehouse glanced up at the grandfather clock.

'Just twelve minutes past eight,' he remarked. 'Joan, I believe you're right, but I never heard the first one. Digby,' he addressed the butler, 'is this the first gong or the second?'

'The first, sir.'

'At twelve minutes past eight? Digby, somebody will get the sack for this.'

A faint smile showed for a minute on the butler's face.

'Dinner is being served ten minutes later tonight, sir. The master's orders.'

'Incredible!' cried Harry Dalehouse. 'Tut, tut! Upon my word, things are coming to a pretty pass! Wonders will never cease. What ails my revered uncle?'

'The seven o'clock train, sir, was half an hour late, and as –' The butler broke off, as a sound like the crack of a whip was heard.

'What on earth –' said Harry. 'Why, that sounded exactly like a shot.'

A dark, handsome man of thirty-five came out of the drawing room on their left.

'What was that?' he asked. 'It sounded exactly like a shot.'

'It must have been a car backfiring, sir,' said the butler. 'The road runs quite close to the house this side and the upstairs windows are open.'

'Perhaps,' said Joan doubtfully. 'But that would be over there.' She waved a hand to the right. 'And I thought the noise came from here.' She pointed to the left.

The dark man shook his head.

'I don't think so. I was in the drawing room. I came out here because I thought the noise came from this direction.' He nodded his head in front of him in the direction of the gong and the front door.

'East, west, and south, eh?' said the irrepressible Harry. 'Well, I'll make it complete, Keene. North for me. I thought it came from behind us. Any solutions offered?'

'Well, there's always murder,' said Geoffrey Keene, smiling. 'I beg your pardon, Miss Ashby.'

'Only a shiver,' said Joan. 'It's nothing. A what-do-you-call-it walking over my grave.'

'A good thought – murder,' said Harry. 'But, alas! No groans, no blood. I fear the solution is a poacher after a rabbit.'

'Seems tame, but I suppose that's it,' agreed the

other. 'But it sounded so near. However, let's come into the drawing room.'

'Thank goodness, we're not late,' said Joan fervently. 'I was simply haring it down the stairs thinking that was the second gong.'

All laughing, they went into the big drawing room.

Lytcham Close was one of the most famous old houses in England. Its owner, Hubert Lytcham Roche, was the last of a long line, and his more distant relatives were apt to remark that 'Old Hubert, you know, really ought to be certified. Mad as a hatter, poor old bird.'

Allowing for the exaggeration natural to friends and relatives, some truth remained. Hubert Lytcham Roche was certainly eccentric. Though a very fine musician, he was a man of ungovernable temper and had an almost abnormal sense of his own importance. People staying in the house had to respect his prejudices or else they were never asked again.

One such prejudice was his music. If he played to his guests, as he often did in the evening, absolute silence must obtain. A whispered comment, a rustle of a dress, a movement even – and he would turn round scowling fiercely, and goodbye to the unlucky guest's chances of being asked again.

Another point was absolute punctuality for the crowning meal of the day. Breakfast was immaterial – you might come down at noon if you wished. Lunch also – a simple meal of cold meats and stewed fruit. But dinner was a rite, a festival, prepared by a *cordon bleu* whom he had tempted from a big hotel by the payment of a fabulous salary.

A first gong was sounded at five minutes past eight. At a quarter past eight a second gong was heard, and immediately after the door was flung open, dinner announced to the assembled guests, and a solemn procession wended its way to the dining room. Anyone who had the temerity to be late for the second gong was henceforth excommunicated – and Lytcham Close shut to the unlucky diner forever.

Hence the anxiety of Joan Ashby, and also the astonishment of Harry Dalehouse, at hearing that the sacred function was to be delayed ten minutes on this particular evening. Though not very intimate with his uncle, he had been to Lytcham Close often enough to know what a very unusual occurrence that was.

Geoffrey Keene, who was Lytcham Roche's secretary, was also very much surprised.

'Extraordinary,' he commented. 'I've never known such a thing to happen. Are you sure?'

'Digby said so.'

'He said something about a train,' said Joan Ashby. 'At least I think so.'

'Queer,' said Keene thoughtfully. 'We shall hear all about it in due course, I suppose. But it's very odd.'

Both men were silent for a moment or two, watching the girl. Joan Ashby was a charming creature, blue-eyed and golden-haired, with an impish glance. This was her first visit to Lytcham Close and her invitation was at Harry's prompting.

The door opened and Diana Cleves, the Lytcham Roches' adopted daughter, came into the room.

There was a daredevil grace about Diana, a witchery in her dark eyes and her mocking tongue. Nearly all men fell for Diana and she enjoyed her conquests. A strange creature, with her alluring suggestion of warmth and her complete coldness.

'Beaten the Old Man for once,' she remarked. 'First time for weeks he hasn't been here first, looking at his watch and tramping up and down like a tiger at feeding time.'

The young men had sprung forward. She smiled entrancingly at them both – then turned to Harry. Geoffrey Keene's dark cheek flushed as he dropped back.

He recovered himself, however, a moment later as Mrs Lytcham Roche came in. She was a tall, dark woman, naturally vague in manner, wearing floating draperies of an indeterminate shade of green. With her was a middle-aged man with a beaklike nose and a determined chin – Gregory Barling. He was a somewhat prominent figure in the financial world and, well-bred on his mother's side, he had for some years been an intimate friend of Hubert Lytcham Roche.

Boom!

The gong resounded imposingly. As it died away, the door was flung open and Digby announced:

'Dinner is served.'

Then, well-trained servant though he was, a look of complete astonishment flashed over his impassive face. For the first time in his memory, his master was not in the room!

That his astonishment was shared by everybody was evident. Mrs Lytcham Roche gave a little uncertain laugh.

'Most amazing. Really – I don't know what to do.'

Everybody was taken aback. The whole tradition of Lytcham Close was undermined. What could have happened? Conversation ceased. There was a strained sense of waiting.

At last the door opened once more; a sigh of relief went round only tempered by a slight anxiety as to how to treat the situation. Nothing must be said to emphasize the fact that the host had himself transgressed the stringent rule of the house.

But the newcomer was not Lytcham Roche. Instead of the big, bearded, viking-like figure, there advanced into the long drawing room a very small man, palpably a foreigner, with an egg-shaped head, a flamboyant moustache, and most irreproachable evening clothes.

His eyes twinkling, the newcomer advanced toward Mrs Lytcham Roche.

'My apologies, madame,' he said. 'I am, I fear, a few minutes late.'

'Oh, not at all!' murmured Mrs Lytcham Roche vaguely. 'Not at all, Mr –' She paused.

'Poirot, madame. Hercule Poirot.'

He heard behind him a very soft 'Oh' – a gasp rather than an articulate word – a woman's ejaculation. Perhaps he was flattered.

'You knew I was coming?' he murmured gently. '*N'est ce pas, madame?* Your husband told you.'

'Oh – oh, yes,' said Mrs Lytcham Roche, her manner unconvincing in the extreme. 'I mean, I suppose so. I am so terribly unpractical, M. Poirot. I never remember anything. But fortunately Digby sees to everything.'

'My train, I fear, was late,' said M. Poirot. 'An accident on the line in front of us.'

'Oh,' cried Joan, 'so that's why dinner was put off.'

His eye came quickly round to her – a most uncannily discerning eye.

'That is something out of the usual – eh?'

'I really can't think –' began Mrs Lytcham Roche, and then stopped. 'I mean,' she went on confusedly, 'it's so odd. Hubert never –'

Poirot's eyes swept rapidly round the group.

'M. Lytcham Roche is not down yet?'

'No, and it's so extraordinary –' She looked appealingly at Geoffrey Keene.

'Mr Lytcham Roche is the soul of punctuality,' explained Keene. 'He has not been late for dinner for – well, I don't know that he was ever late before.'

To a stranger the situation must have been ludicrous – the perturbed faces and the general consternation.

'I know,' said Mrs Lytcham Roche with the air of one solving a problem. 'I shall ring for Digby.'

She suited the action to the word.

The butler came promptly.

'Digby,' said Mrs Lytcham Roche, 'your master. Is he –'

As was customary with her, she did not finish her sentence. It was clear that the butler did not expect her to do so. He replied promptly and with understanding.

'Mr Lytcham Roche came down at five minutes to eight and went into the study, madam.'

'Oh!' She paused. 'You don't think – I mean – he heard the gong?'

'I think he must have – the gong is immediately outside the study door.'

'Yes, of course, of course,' said Mrs Lytcham Roche more vaguely than ever.

'Shall I inform him, madam, that dinner is ready?'

'Oh, thank you, Digby. Yes, I think – yes, yes, I should.'

'I don't know,' said Mrs Lytcham Roche to her guests as the butler withdrew, 'what I would do without Digby!'

A pause followed.

Then Digby re-entered the room. His breath was coming a little faster than is considered good form in a butler.

'Excuse me, madam – the study door is locked.'

It was then that M. Hercule Poirot took command of the situation.

'I think,' he said, 'that we had better go to the study.'

He led the way and everyone followed. His assumption of authority seemed perfectly natural. he was no longer a rather comic-looking guest. He was a personality and master of the situation.

He led the way out into the hall, past the staircase, past the great clock, past the recess in which stood the gong. Exactly opposite that recess was a closed door.

He tapped on it, first gently, then with increasing violence. But there was no reply. Very nimbly he dropped to his knees and applied his eye to the keyhole. He rose and looked round.

'Messieurs,' he said, 'we must break open this door. Immediately!'

As before no one questioned his authority. Geoffrey

Keene and Gregory Barling were the two biggest men. They attacked the door under Poirot's directions. It was no easy matter. The doors of Lytcham Close were solid affairs – no modern jerry-building here. It resisted the attack valiantly, but at last it gave before the united attack of the men and crashed inward.

The house party hesitated in the doorway. They saw what they had subconsciously feared to see. Facing them was the window. On the left, between the door and the window, was a big writing table. Sitting, not at the table, but sideways to it, was a man – a big man – slouched forward in the chair. His back was to them and his face to the window, but his position told the tale. His right hand hung limply down and below it, on the carpet, was a small shining pistol.

Poirot spoke sharply to Gregory Barling.

'Take Mrs Lytcham Roche away – and the other two ladies.'

The other nodded comprehendingly. He laid a hand on his hostess's arm. She shivered.

'He has shot himself,' she murmured. 'Horrible!' With another shiver she permitted him to lead her away. The two girls followed.

Poirot came forward into the room, the two young men behind him.

He knelt down by the body, motioning them to keep back a little.

He found the bullet hole on the right side of the head. It had passed out the other side and had evidently struck a mirror hanging on the left-hand wall, since this was shivered. On the writing table was a sheet of paper, blank save for the word *Sorry* scrawled across it in hesitating, shaky writing.

Poirot's eyes darted back to the door.

'The key is not in the lock,' he said. 'I wonder –'

His hand slid into the dead man's pocket.

'Here it is,' he said. 'At least I think so. Have the goodness to try it, monsieur?'

Geoffrey Keene took it from him and tried it in the lock.

'That's it, all right.'

'And the window?'

Harry Dalehouse strode across to it.

'Shut.'

'You permit?' Very swiftly, Poirot scrambled to his feet and joined the other at the window. It was a long French window. Poirot opened it, stood a minute scrutinizing the grass just in front of it, then closed it again.

'My friends,' he said, 'we must telephone for the police. Until they have come and satisfied themselves that it is truly suicide nothing must be touched. Death can only have occurred about a quarter of an hour ago.'

'I know,' said Harry hoarsely. 'We heard the shot.'

'*Comment?* What is that you say?'

Harry explained with the help of Geoffrey Keene. As he finished speaking, Barling reappeared.

Poirot repeated what he had said before, and while Keene went off to telephone, Poirot requested Barling to give him a few minutes' interview.

They went into a small morning room, leaving Digby on guard outside the study door, while Harry went off to find the ladies.

'You were, I understand, an intimate friend of M. Lytcham Roche,' began Poirot. 'It is for that reason that I address myself to you primarily. In etiquette, perhaps, I should have spoken first to madame, but at the moment I do not think that is *pratique*.'

He paused.

'I am, see you, in a delicate situation. I will lay the facts plainly before you. I am, by profession, a private detective.'

The financier smiled a little.

'It is not necessary to tell me that, M. Poirot. Your name is, by now, a household word.'

'Monsieur is too amiable,' said Poirot, bowing. 'Let us, then, proceed. I receive, at my London address, a letter from this M. Lytcham Roche. In it he says that he has reason to believe that he is being swindled of large sums of money. For family reasons, so he puts it, he does not wish to call in the police, but he desires that

I should come down and look into the matter for him. Well, I agree. I come. Not quite so soon as M. Lytcham Roche wishes – for after all I have other affairs, and M. Lytcham Roche, he is not quite the King of England, though he seems to think he is.'

Barling gave a wry smile.

'He did think of himself that way.'

'Exactly. Oh, you comprehend – his letter showed plainly enough that he was what one calls an eccentric. He was not insane, but he was unbalanced, *n'est-ce pas?*'

'What he's just done ought to show that.'

'Oh, monsieur, but suicide is not always the act of the unbalanced. The coroner's jury, they say so, but that is to spare the feelings of those left behind.'

'Hubert was not a normal individual,' said Barling decisively. 'He was given to ungovernable rages, was a monomaniac on the subject of family pride, and had a bee in his bonnet in more ways than one. But for all that he was a shrewd man.'

'Precisely. He was sufficiently shrewd to discover that he was being robbed.'

'Does a man commit suicide because he's being robbed?' Barling asked.

'As you say, monsieur. Ridiculous. And that brings me to the need for haste in the matter. For family reasons – that was the phrase he used in his letter. *Eh bien*, monsieur, you are a man of the world, you know that it is for precisely that – family reasons – that a man does commit suicide.'

'You mean?'

'That it looks – on the face of it – as if *ce pauvre* monsieur had found out something further – and was unable to face what he had found out. But you perceive, I have a duty. I am already employed – commissioned – I have accepted the task. This "family reason", the dead man did not want it to get to the police. So I must act quickly. I must learn the truth.'

'And when you have learned it?'

'Then – I must use my discretion. I must do what I can.'

'I see,' said Barling. He smoked for a minute or two in silence, then he said, 'All the same I'm afraid I can't help you. Hubert never confided anything to me. I know nothing.'

'But tell me, monsieur, who, should you say, had a chance of robbing this poor gentleman?'

'Difficult to say. Of course, there's the agent for the estate. He's a new man.'

'The agent?'

'Yes. Marshall. Captain Marshall. Very nice fellow, lost an arm in the war. He came here a year ago. But Hubert liked him, I know, and trusted him, too.'

'If it were Captain Marshall who was playing him false, there would be no family reasons for silence.'

'N-No.'

The hesitation did not escape Poirot.

'Speak, monsieur. Speak plainly, I beg of you.'

'It may be gossip.'

'I implore you, speak.'

'Very well, then, I will. Did you notice a very attractive looking young woman in the drawing room?'

'I noticed two very attractive looking young women.'

'Oh, yes, Miss Ashby. Pretty little thing. Her first visit. Harry Dalehouse got Mrs Lytcham Roche to ask her. No, I mean a dark girl – Diana Cleves.'

'I noticed her,' said Poirot. 'She is one that all men would notice, I think.'

'She's a little devil,' burst out Barling. 'She's played fast and loose with every man for twenty miles round. Someone will murder her one of these days.'

He wiped his brow with a handkerchief, oblivious of the keen interest with which the other was regarding him.

'And this young lady is –'

'She's Lytcham Roche's adopted daughter. A great disappointment when he and his wife had no children. They adopted Diana Cleves – she was some kind of cousin. Hubert was devoted to her, simply worshipped her.'

'Doubtless he would dislike the idea of her marrying?' suggested Poirot.

'Not if she married the right person.'

'And the right person was – you, monsieur?'

Barling started and flushed.

'I never said –'

'*Mais, non, mais, non!* You said nothing. But it was so, was it not?'

'I fell in love with her – yes. Lytcham Roche was pleased about it. It fitted in with his ideas for her.'

'And mademoiselle herself?'

'I told you – she's the devil incarnate.'

'I comprehend. She has her own ideas of amusement, is it not so? But Captain Marshall, where does he come in?'

'Well, she's been seeing a lot of him. People talked. Not that I think there's anything in it. Another scalp, that's all.'

Poirot nodded.

'But supposing that there had been something in it – well, then, it might explain why M. Lytcham Roche wanted to proceed cautiously.'

'You do understand, don't you, that there's no earthly reason for suspecting Marshall of defalcation.'

'*Oh, parfaitement, parfaitement!* It might be an affair of a forged cheque with someone in the household involved. This young Mr Dalehouse, who is he?'

'A nephew.'

'He will inherit, yes?'

'He's a sister's son. Of course he might take the name – there's not a Lytcham Roche left.'

'I see.'

'The place isn't actually entailed, though it's always gone from father to son. I've always imagined that he'd leave the place to his wife for her lifetime and then perhaps to Diana if he approved of her marriage. You see, her husband could take the name.'

'I comprehend,' said Poirot. 'You have been most kind and helpful to me, monsieur. May I ask of you one thing further – to explain to Madame Lytcham Roche all that I have told you, and to beg of her that she accord me a minute?'

Sooner than he had thought likely, the door opened and Mrs Lytcham Roche entered. She floated to a chair.

'Mr Barling has explained everything to me,' she said. 'We mustn't have any scandal, of course. Though I do feel really it's fate, don't you? I mean with the mirror and everything.'

'*Comment* – the mirror?'

'The moment I saw it – it seemed a symbol. Of Hubert! A curse, you know. I think old families have a curse very often. Hubert was always very strange. Lately he has been stranger than ever.'

'You will forgive me for asking, madame, but you are not in any way short of money?'

'Money? I never think of money.'

'Do you know what they say, madame? Those who never think of money need a great deal of it.'

He ventured a tiny laugh. She did not respond. Her eyes were far away.

'I thank you, madame,' he said, and the interview came to an end.

Poirot rang, and Digby answered.

'I shall require you to answer a few questions,' said Poirot. 'I am a private detective sent for by your master before he died.'

'A detective!' the butler gasped. 'Why?'

'You will please answer my questions. As to the shot now –'

He listened to the butler's account.

'So there were four of you in the hall?'

'Yes, sir; Mr Dalehouse and Miss Ashby and Mr Keene came from the drawing room.'

'Where were the others?'

'The others, sir?'

'Yes, Mrs Lytcham Roche, Miss Cleves and Mr Barling.'

'Mrs Lytcham Roche and Mr Barling came down later, sir.'

'And Miss Cleves?'

'I think Miss Cleves was in the drawing room, sir.'

Poirot asked a few more questions, then dismissed

the butler with the command to request Miss Cleves to come to him.

She came immediately, and he studied her attentively in view of Barling's revelations. She was certainly beautiful in her white satin frock with the rosebud on the shoulder.

He explained the circumstances which had brought him to Lytcham Close, eyeing her very closely, but she showed only what seemed to be genuine astonishment, with no signs of uneasiness. She spoke of Marshall indifferently with tepid approval. Only at mention of Barling did she approach animation.

'That man's a crook,' she said sharply. 'I told the Old Man so, but he wouldn't listen – went on putting money into his rotten concerns.'

'Are you sorry, mademoiselle, that your – father is dead?'

She stared at him.

'Of course. I'm modern, you know, M. Poirot. I don't indulge in sob stuff. But I was fond of the Old Man. Though, of course, it's best for him.'

'Best for him?'

'Yes. One of these days he would have had to be locked up. It was growing on him – this belief that the last Lytcham Roche of Lytcham Close was omnipotent.'

Poirot nodded thoughtfully.

'I see, I see – yes, decided signs of mental trouble. By the way, you permit that I examine your little bag? It is charming – all these silk rosebuds. What was I saying? Oh, yes, did you hear the shot?'

'Oh, yes! But I thought it was a car or a poacher, or something.'

'You were in the drawing room?'

'No. I was out in the garden.'

'I see. Thank you, mademoiselle. Next I would like to see M. Keene, is it not?'

'Geoffrey? I'll send him along.'

Keene came in, alert and interested.

'Mr Barling has been telling me of the reason for your being down here. I don't know that there's anything I can tell you, but if I can –'

Poirot interrupted him. 'I only want to know one thing, Monsieur Keene. What was it that you stooped and picked up just before we got to the study door this evening?'

'I –' Keene half sprang up from his chair, then subsided again. 'I don't know what you mean,' he said lightly.

'Oh, I think you do, monsieur. You were behind me, I know, but a friend of mine he says I have eyes in the back of my head. You picked up something and you put it in the right hand pocket of your dinner jacket.'

There was a pause. Indecision was written plainly

on Keene's handsome face. At last he made up his mind.

'Take your choice, M. Poirot,' he said, and leaning forward he turned his pocket inside out. There was a cigarette holder, a handkerchief, a tiny silk rosebud, and a little gold match box.

A moment's silence and then Keene said, 'As a matter of fact it was this.' He picked up the match box. 'I must have dropped it earlier in the evening.'

'I think not,' said Poirot.

'What do you mean?'

'What I say. I, monsieur, am a man of tidiness, of method, of order. A match box on the ground, I should see it and pick it up – a match box of this size, assuredly I should see it! No, monsieur, I think it was something very much smaller – such as this, perhaps.'

He picked up the little silk rosebud.

'From Miss Cleve's bag, I think?'

There was a moment's pause, then Keene admitted it with a laugh.

'Yes, that's so. She – gave it to me last night.'

'I see,' said Poirot, and at the moment the door opened and a tall fair-haired man in a lounge suit strode into the room.

'Keene – what's all this? Lytcham Roche shot himself? Man, I can't believe it. It's incredible.'

'Let me introduce you,' said Keene, 'to M. Hercule

Poirot.' The other started. 'He will tell you all about it.' And he left the room, banging the door.

'M. Poirot –' John Marshall was all eagerness '– I'm most awfully pleased to meet you. It is a bit of luck your being down here. Lytcham Roche never told me you were coming. I'm a most frightful admirer of yours, sir.'

A disarming young man, thought Poirot – not so young, either, for there was grey hair at the temples and lines in the forehead. It was the voice and manner that gave the impression of boyishness.

'The police –'

'They are here now, sir. I came up with them on hearing the news. They don't seem particularly surprised. Of course, he was mad as a hatter, but even then –'

'Even then you are surprised at his committing suicide?'

'Frankly, yes. I shouldn't have thought that – well, that Lytcham Roche could have imagined the world getting on without him.'

'He has had money troubles of late, I understand?'

Marshall nodded.

'He speculated. Wildcat schemes of Barling's.'

Poirot said quietly, 'I will be very frank. Had you any reason to suppose that Mr Lytcham Roche suspected you of tampering with your accounts?'

Marshall stared at Poirot in a kind of ludicrous bewilderment. So ludicrous was it that Poirot was forced to smile.

'I see that you are utterly taken aback, Captain Marshall.'

'Yes, indeed. The idea's ridiculous.'

'Ah! Another question. He did not suspect you of robbing him of his adopted daughter?'

'Oh, so you know about me and Di?' He laughed in an embarrassed fashion.

'It is so, then?'

Marshall nodded.

'But the old man didn't know anything about it. Di wouldn't have him told. I suppose she was right. He'd have gone up like a – a basketful of rockets. I should have been chucked out of a job, and that would have been that.'

'And instead what was your plan?'

'Well, upon my word, sir, I hardly know. I left things to Di. She said she'd fix it. As a matter of fact I was looking out for a job. If I could have got one I would have chucked this up.'

'And mademoiselle would have married you? But M. Lytcham Roche might have stopped her allowance. Mademoiselle Diana is, I should say, fond of money.'

Marshall looked rather uncomfortable.

'I'd have tried to make it up to her, sir.'

Geoffrey Keene came into the room. 'The police are just going and would like to see you, M. Poirot.'

'*Merci.* I will come.'

In the study were a stalwart inspector and the police surgeon.

'Mr Poirot?' said the inspector. 'We've heard of you, sir. I'm Inspector Reeves.'

'You are most amiable,' said Poirot, shaking hands. 'You do not need my co-operation, no?' He gave a little laugh.

'Not this time, sir. All plain sailing.'

'The case is perfectly straightforward, then?' demanded Poirot.

'Absolutely. Door and window locked, key of door in dead man's pocket. Manner very strange the past few days. No doubt about it.'

'Everything quite – natural?'

The doctor grunted.

'Must have been sitting at a damned queer angle for the bullet to have hit that mirror. But suicide's a queer business.'

'You found the bullet?'

'Yes, here.' The doctor held it out. 'Near the wall below the mirror. Pistol was Mr Roche's own. Kept it in the drawer of the desk always. Something behind it all, I daresay, but what that is we shall never know.'

Poirot nodded.

The body had been carried to a bedroom. The police now took their leave. Poirot stood at the front door looking after them. A sound made him turn. Harry Dalehouse was close behind him.

'Have you, by any chance, a strong flashlight, my friend?' asked Poirot.

'Yes, I'll get it for you.'

When he returned with it Joan Ashby was with him.

'You may accompany me if you like,' said Poirot graciously.

He stepped out of the front door and turned to the right, stopping before the study window. About six feet of grass separated it from the path. Poirot bent down, playing the flashlight on the grass. He straightened himself and shook his head.

'No,' he said, 'not there.'

Then he paused and slowly his figure stiffened. On either side of the grass was a deep flower border. Poirot's attention was focused on the right hand border, full of Michaelmas daisies and dahlias. His torch was directed on the front of the bed. Distinct on the soft mould were footprints.

'Four of them,' murmured Poirot. 'Two going toward the window, two coming from it.'

'A gardener,' suggested Joan.

'But no, mademoiselle, but no. Employ your eyes. These shoes are small, dainty, high-heeled, the shoes of a woman. Mademoiselle Diana mentioned having been out in the garden. Do you know if she went downstairs before you did, mademoiselle?'

Joan shook her head.

'I can't remember. I was in such a hurry because the gong went, and I thought I'd heard the first one. I do seem to remember that her room door was open as I went past, but I'm not sure. Mrs Lytcham Roche's was shut, I know.'

'I see,' said Poirot.

Something in his voice made Harry look up sharply, but Poirot was merely frowning gently to himself.

In the doorway they met Diana Cleves.

'The police have gone,' she said. 'It's all – over.'

She gave a deep sigh.

'May I request one little word with you, mademoiselle?'

She led the way into the morning room, and Poirot followed, shutting the door.

'Well?' She looked a little surprised.

'One little question, mademoiselle. Were you tonight at any time in the flower border outside the study window?'

'Yes.' She nodded. 'About seven o'clock and again just before dinner.'

'I do not understand,' he said.

'I can't see that there is anything to "understand", as

you call it,' she said coldly. 'I was picking Michaelmas daisies – for the table. I always do the flowers. That was about seven o'clock.'

'And afterward – later?'

'Oh, that! As a matter of fact I dropped a spot of hair oil on my dress – just on the shoulder here. It was just as I was ready to come down. I didn't want to change the dress. I remembered I'd seen a late rose in bud in the border. I ran out and picked it and pinned it in. See –' She came close to him and lifted the head of the rose. Poirot saw the minute grease spot. She remained close to him, her shoulder almost brushing his.

'And what time was this?'

'Oh, about ten minutes past eight, I suppose.'

'You did not – try the window?'

'I believe I did. Yes, I thought it would be quicker to go in that way. But it was fastened.'

'I see.' Poirot drew a deep breath. 'And the shot,' he said, 'where were you when you heard that? Still in the flower border?'

'Oh, no; it was two or three minutes later, just before I came in by the side door.'

'Do you know what this is, mademoiselle?'

On the palm of his hand he held out the tiny silk rosebud. She examined it coolly.

'It looks like a rosebud off my little evening bag. Where did you find it?'

'It was in Mr Keene's pocket,' said Poirot dryly. 'Did you give it to him, mademoiselle?'

'Did he tell you I gave it to him?'

Poirot smiled.

'When did you give it to him, mademoiselle?'

'Last night.'

'Did he warn you to say that, mademoiselle?'

'What do you mean?' she asked angrily.

But Poirot did not answer. He strode out of the room and into the drawing room. Barling, Keene, and Marshall were there. He went straight up to them.

'Messieurs,' he said brusquely, 'will you follow me to the study?'

He passed out into the hall and addressed Joan and Harry.

'You, too, I pray of you. And will somebody request madame to come? I thank you. Ah! And here is the excellent Digby. Digby, a little question, a very important little question. Did Miss Cleves arrange some Michaelmas daisies before dinner?'

The butler looked bewildered.

'Yes, sir, she did.'

'You are sure?'

'Quite sure, sir.'

'*Très bien*. Now – come, all of you.'

Inside the study he faced them.

'I have asked you to come here for a reason. The

case is over, the police have come and gone. They say Mr Lytcham Roche has shot himself. All is finished.' He paused. 'But I, Hercule Poirot, say that it is not finished.'

As startled eyes turned to him the door opened and Mrs Lytcham Roche floated into the room.

'I was saying, madame, that this case is not finished. It is a matter of the psychology. Mr Lytcham Roche, he had the *manie de grandeur*, he was a king. Such a man does not kill himself. No, no, he may go mad, but he does not kill himself. Mr Lytcham Roche did not kill himself.' He paused. 'He was killed.'

'Killed?' Marshall gave a short laugh. 'Alone in a room with the door and window locked?'

'All the same,' said Poirot stubbornly, 'he was killed.'

'And got up and locked the door or shut the window afterward, I suppose,' said Diana cuttingly.

'I will show you something,' said Poirot, going to the window. He turned the handle of the French windows and then pulled gently.

'See, they are open. Now I close them, but without turning the handle. Now the window is closed but not fastened. Now!'

He gave a short jarring blow and the handle turned, shooting the bolt down into its socket.

'You see?' said Poirot softly. 'It is very loose, this mechanism. It could be done from outside quite easily.'

He turned, his manner grim.

'When that shot was fired at twelve minutes past eight, there were four people in the hall. Four people have an alibi. Where were the other three? You, madame? In your room. You, Monsieur Barling. Were you, too, in your room?'

'I was.'

'And you, mademoiselle, were in the garden. So you have admitted.'

'I don't see –' began Diana.

'Wait.' He turned to Mrs Lytcham Roche. 'Tell me, madame, have you any idea of how your husband left his money?'

'Hubert read me his will. He said I ought to know. He left me three thousand a year chargeable on the estate, and the dower house or the town house, whichever I preferred. Everything else he left to Diana, on condition that if she married her husband must take the name.'

'Ah!'

'But then he made a codicil thing – a few weeks ago, that was.'

'Yes, madame?'

'He still left it all to Diana, but on condition that she married Mr Barling. If she married anyone else, it was all to go to his nephew, Harry Dalehouse.'

'But the codicil was only made a few weeks ago,' purred Poirot. 'Mademoiselle may not have known of that.' He stepped forward accusingly. 'Mademoiselle Diana, you want to marry Captain Marshall, do you not? Or is it Mr Keene?'

She walked across the room and put her arm through Marshall's sound one.

'Go on,' she said.

'I will put the case against you, mademoiselle. You loved Captain Marshall. You also loved money. Your adopted father he would never have consented to your marrying Captain Marshall, but if he dies you are fairly sure that you get everything. So you go out, you step over the flower border to the window which is open, you have with you the pistol which you have taken from the writing table drawer. You go up to your victim talking amiably. You fire. You drop the pistol by his hand, having wiped it and then pressed his fingers on it. You go out again, shaking the window till the bolt drops. You come into the house. Is that how it happened? I am asking you, mademoiselle?'

'No,' Diana screamed. 'No – no!'

He looked at her, then he smiled.

'No,' he said, 'it was not like that. It might have been so – it is plausible – it is possible – but it cannot have been like that for two reasons. The first reason is that you picked Michaelmas daisies at seven o'clock, the second arises from something that mademoiselle here told me.' He turned toward Joan, who stared at him in bewilderment. He nodded encouragement.

'But yes, mademoiselle. You told me that you hurried downstairs because you thought it was the second gong sounding, having already heard the first.'

He shot a rapid glance round the room.

'You do not see what that means?' he cried. 'You do not see. Look! Look!' He sprang forward to the chair where the victim had sat. 'Did you notice how the body was? Not sitting square to the desk – no, sitting sideways to the desk, facing the window. Is that a natural way to commit suicide? *Jamais, jamais!* You write your apologia "sorry" on a piece of paper – you open the drawer, you take out the pistol, you hold it to your head and you fire. That is the way of suicide. But now consider murder! The victim sits at his desk, the murderer stands beside him – talking. And talking still – fires. Where does the bullet go then?' He paused. 'Straight through the head, through the door if it is open, and so – hits the gong.

'Ah! you begin to see? That was the first gong – heard only by mademoiselle, since her room is above.

'What does our murderer do next? Shuts the door, locks it, puts the key in the dead man's pocket, then turns the body sideways in the chair, presses the dead man's fingers on the pistol and then drops it by his side, cracks the mirror on the wall as a final spectacular touch

– in short, "arranges" his suicide. Then out through the window, the bolt is shaken home, the murderer steps not on the grass, where footprints must show, but on the flower bed, where they can be smoothed out behind him, leaving no trace. Then back into the house, and at twelve minutes past eight, when he is alone in the drawing room, he fires a service revolver out of the drawing room window and dashes out into the hall. Is that how you did it, Mr Geoffrey Keene?'

Fascinated, the secretary stared at the accusing figure drawing nearer to him. Then, with a gurgling cry, he fell to the ground.

'I think I am answered,' said Poirot. 'Captain Marshall, will you ring up the police?' He bent over the prostrate form. 'I fancy he will be still unconscious when they come.'

'Geoffrey Keene,' murmured Diana. 'But what motive had he?'

'I fancy that as secretary he had certain opportunities – accounts – cheques. Something awakened Mr Lytcham Roche's suspicions. He sent for me.'

'Why for you? Why not for the police?'

'I think, mademoiselle, you can answer that question. Monsieur suspected that there was something between you and that young man. To divert his mind from Captain Marshall, you had flirted shamelessly with Mr Keene. But yes, you need not deny! Mr Keene gets wind of my coming and acts promptly. The essence of his scheme is that the crime must seem to take place at 8:12, when he has an alibi. His one danger is the bullet, which must be lying somewhere near the gong and which he has not had time to retrieve. When we are all on our way to the study he picks that up. At such a tense moment he thinks no one will notice. But me, I notice everything! I question him. He reflects a little minute and then he plays the comedy! He insinuates that what he picked up was the silk rosebud, he plays the part of the young man in love shielding the lady he loves. Oh, it was very clever, and if you had not picked Michaelmas daisies –'

'I don't understand what they have to do with it.'

'You do not? Listen – there were only four footprints in the bed, but when you were picking the flowers you must have made many more than that. So in between your picking the flowers and your coming to get the rosebud someone must have smoothed over the bed. Not a gardener – no gardener works after seven. Then it must be someone guilty – it must be the murderer – the murder was committed before the shot was heard.'

'But why did nobody hear the real shot?' asked Harry.

'A silencer. They will find that and the revolver thrown into the shrubbery.'

'What a risk!'

'Why a risk? Everyone was upstairs dressing for dinner. It was a very good moment. The bullet was the only contretemps, and even that, as he thought, passed off well.'

Poirot picked it up. 'He threw it under the mirror when I was examining the window with Mr Dalehouse.'

'Oh!' Diana wheeled on Marshall. 'Marry me, John, and take me away.'

Barling coughed. 'My dear Diana, under the terms of my friend's will –'

'I don't care,' the girl cried. 'We can draw pictures on pavements.'

'There's no need to do that,' said Harry. 'We'll go halves, Di. I'm not going to bag things because Uncle had a bee in his bonnet.'

Suddenly there was a cry. Mrs Lytcham Roche had sprung to her feet.

'M. Poirot – the mirror – he – he must have deliberately smashed it.'

'Yes, madame.'

'Oh!' She stared at him. 'But it is unlucky to break a mirror.'

'It has proved very unlucky for Mr Geoffrey Keene,' said Poirot cheerfully.

Yellow Iris

I

Hercule Poirot stretched out his feet towards the electric radiator set in the wall. Its neat arrangement of red hot bars pleased his orderly mind.

'A coal fire,' he mused to himself, 'was always shapeless and haphazard! Never did it achieve the symmetry.'

The telephone bell rang. Poirot rose, glancing at his watch as he did so. The time was close on half past eleven. He wondered who was ringing him up at this hour. It might, of course, be a wrong number.

'And it might,' he murmured to himself with a whimsical smile, 'be a millionaire newspaper proprietor, found dead in the library of his country house, with a spotted orchid clasped in his left hand and a page torn from a cookbook pinned to his breast.'

Smiling at the pleasing conceit, he lifted the receiver.

Immediately a voice spoke – a soft husky woman's voice with a kind of desperate urgency about it.

'*Is that M. Hercule Poirot? Is that M. Hercule Poirot?*'

'Hercule Poirot speaks.'

'*M. Poirot – can you come at once – at once – I'm in danger – in great danger – I know it . . .*'

Poirot said sharply:

'Who are you? Where are you speaking from?'

The voice came more faintly but with an even greater urgency.

'*At once . . . it's life or death . . . the Jardin des Cygnes . . . at once . . . table with yellow irises . . .*'

There was a pause – a queer kind of gasp – the line went dead.

Hercule Poirot hung up. His face was puzzled. He murmured between his teeth:

'There is something here very curious.'

II

In the doorway of the Jardin des Cygnes, fat Luigi hurried forward.

'*Buona sera*, M. Poirot. You desire a table – yes?'

'No, no, my good Luigi. I seek here for some friends. I will look round – perhaps they are not here yet. Ah, let me see, that table there in the corner with the yellow irises – a little question by the way, if it is not indiscreet. On all the other tables there are tulips – pink tulips – why on that one table do you have yellow irises?'

Luigi shrugged his expressive shoulders.

'A command, Monsieur! A special order! Without doubt, the favourite flowers of one of the ladies. That table it is the table of Mr Barton Russell – an American – immensely rich.'

'Aha, one must study the whims of the ladies, must one not, Luigi?'

'Monsieur has said it,' said Luigi.

'I see at that table an acquaintance of mine. I must go and speak to him.'

Poirot skirted his way delicately round the dancing floor on which couples were revolving. The table in question was set for six, but it had at the moment only one occupant, a young man who was thoughtfully, and it seemed pessimistically, drinking champagne.

He was not at all the person that Poirot had expected to see. It seemed impossible to associate the idea of danger or melodrama with any party of which Tony Chapell was a member.

Poirot paused delicately by the table.

'Ah, it is, is it not, my friend Anthony Chapell?'

'By all that's wonderful – Poirot, the police hound!' cried the young man. 'Not Anthony, my dear fellow – Tony to friends!'

He drew out a chair.

'Come, sit with me. Let us discourse of crime! Let us go further and drink to crime.' He poured champagne into an empty glass. 'But what are you doing in this haunt of song and dance and merriment, my dear Poirot? We have no bodies here, positively not a single body to offer you.'

Poirot sipped the champagne.

'You seem very gay, *mon cher?*'

'Gay? I am steeped in misery – wallowing in gloom. Tell me, you hear this tune they are playing. You recognize it?'

Poirot hazarded cautiously:

'Something perhaps to do with your baby having left you?'

'Not a bad guess,' said the young man, 'but wrong for once. "There's nothing like love for making you miserable!" That's what it's called.'

'Aha?'

'My favourite tune,' said Tony Chapell mournfully. 'And my favourite restaurant and my favourite band – and my favourite girl's here and she's dancing it with somebody else.'

'Hence the melancholy?' said Poirot.

'Exactly. Pauline and I, you see, have had what the vulgar call words. That is to say, she's had ninety-five words to five of mine out of every hundred. My five are: "*But, darling – I can explain.*" – Then she starts in on her ninety-five again and we get no further. I think,' added Tony sadly, 'that I shall poison myself.'

'Pauline?' murmured Poirot.

'Pauline Weatherby. Barton Russell's young sister-in-law. Young, lovely, disgustingly rich. Tonight Barton Russell gives a party. You know him? Big Business, clean-shaven American – full of pep and personality. His wife was Pauline's sister.'

'And who else is there at this party?'

'You'll meet 'em in a minute when the music stops. There's Lola Valdez – you know, the South American dancer in the new show at the Metropole, and there's Stephen Carter. D'you know Carter – he's in the diplomatic service. Very hush-hush. Known as silent Stephen. Sort of man who says, "*I am not at liberty to state, etc, etc.*" Hullo, here they come.'

Poirot rose. He was introduced to Barton Russell, to Stephen Carter, to Señora Lola Valdez, a dark and luscious creature, and to Pauline Weatherby, very young, very fair, with eyes like cornflowers.

Barton Russell said:

'What, is this the great M. Hercule Poirot? I am indeed pleased to meet you sir. Won't you sit down and join us? That is, unless –'

Tony Chapell broke in.

'He's got an appointment with a body, I believe,

or is it an absconding financier, or the Rajah of Borrioboolagah's great ruby?'

'Ah, my friend, do you think I am never off duty? Can I not, for once, seek only to amuse myself?'

'Perhaps you've got an appointment with Carter here. The latest from the UN International situation now acute. The stolen plans *must* be found or war will be declared tomorrow!'

Pauline Weatherby said cuttingly:

'Must you be so *completely* idiotic, Tony?'

'Sorry, Pauline.'

Tony Chapell relapsed into crestfallen silence.

'How severe you are, Mademoiselle.'

'I hate people who play the fool all the time!'

'I must be careful, I see. I must converse only of serious matters.'

'Oh, no, M. Poirot. I didn't mean you.'

She turned a smiling face to him and asked:

'Are you really a kind of Sherlock Holmes and do wonderful deductions?'

'Ah, the deductions – they are not so easy in real life. But shall I try? Now then, I deduce – that yellow irises are your favourite flowers?'

'Quite wrong, M. Poirot. Lilies of the valley or roses.'

Poirot sighed.

'A failure. I will try once more. This evening, not very long ago, you telephoned to someone.'

Pauline laughed and clapped her hands.

'Quite right.'

'It was not long after you arrived here?'

'Right again. I telephoned the minute I got inside the doors.'

'Ah – that is not so good. You telephoned *before* you came to this table?'

'Yes.'

'Decidedly very bad.'

'Oh, no, I think it was very clever of you. How did you know I had telephoned?'

'That, Mademoiselle, is the great detective's secret. And the person to whom you telephoned – does the name begin with a P – or perhaps with an H?'

Pauline laughed.

'Quite wrong. I telephoned to my maid to post some frightfully important letters that I'd never sent off. Her name's Louise.'

'I am confused – quite confused.'

The music began again.

'What about it, Pauline?' asked Tony.

'I don't think I want to dance again so soon, Tony.'

'Isn't that too bad?' said Tony bitterly to the world at large.

Poirot murmured to the South American girl on his other side:

'Señora, I would not dare to ask you to dance with me. I am too much of the antique.'

Lola Valdez said:

'Ah, it ees nonsense that you talk there! You are steel young. Your hair, eet is still black!'

Poirot winced slightly.

'Pauline, as your brother-in-law and your guardian,' Barton Russell spoke heavily, 'I'm just going to force you onto the floor! This one's a waltz and a waltz is about the only dance I really can do.'

'Why, of course, Barton, we'll take the floor right away.'

'Good girl, Pauline, that's swell of you.'

They went off together. Tony tipped back his chair. Then he looked at Stephen Carter.

'Talkative little fellow, aren't you, Carter?' he remarked. 'Help to make a party go with your merry chatter, eh, what?'

'Really, Chapell, I don't know what you mean?'

'Oh, you don't – don't you?' Tony mimicked him.

'My dear fellow.'

'Drink, man, drink, if you won't talk.'

'No, thanks.'

'Then I will.'

Stephen Carter shrugged his shoulders.

'Excuse me, must just speak to a fellow I know over there. Fellow I was with at Eton.'

Stephen Carter got up and walked to a table a few places away.

Tony said gloomily:

'Somebody ought to drown old Etonians at birth.'

Hercule Poirot was still being gallant to the dark beauty beside him.

He murmured:

'I wonder, may I ask, what are the favourite flowers of Mademoiselle?'

'Ah, now, why ees eet you want to know?'

Lola was arch.

'Mademoiselle, if I send flowers to a lady, I am particular that they should be flowers she likes.'

'That ees very charming of you, M. Poirot. I weel tell you – I adore the big dark red carnations – or the dark red roses.'

'Superb – yes, superb! You do not, then, like yellow irises?'

'Yellow flowers – no – they do not accord with my temperament.'

'How wise . . . Tell me, Mademoiselle, did you ring up a friend tonight, since you arrived here?'

'I? Ring up a friend? No, what a curious question!'

'Ah, but I, I am a very curious man.'

'I'm sure you are.' She rolled her dark eyes at him. 'A vairy *dan*gerous man.'

'No, no, not dangerous; say, a man who may be useful – in danger! You understand?'

Lola giggled. She showed white even teeth.

'No, no,' she laughed. 'You are dangerous.'

Hercule Poirot sighed.

'I see that you do not understand. All this is very strange.'

Tony came out of a fit of abstraction and said suddenly:

'Lola, what about a spot of swoop and dip? Come along.'

'I weel come – yes. Since M. Poirot ees not brave enough!'

Tony put an arm round her and remarked over his shoulder to Poirot as they glided off:

'You can meditate on crime yet to come, old boy!'

Poirot said: 'It is profound what you say there. Yes, it is profound . . .'

He sat meditatively for a minute or two, then he raised a finger. Luigi came promptly, his wide Italian face wreathed in smiles.

'*Mon vieux*,' said Poirot. 'I need some information.'

'Always at your service, Monsieur.'

'I desire to know how many of these people at this table here have used the telephone tonight?'

'I can tell you, Monsieur. The young lady, the one in white, she telephoned at once when she got here.

Then she went to leave her cloak and while she was doing that the other lady came out of the cloakroom and went into the telephone box.'

'So the Señora *did* telephone! Was that *before* she came into the restaurant?'

'Yes, Monsieur.'

'Anyone else?'

'No, Monsieur.'

'All this, Luigi, gives me furiously to think!'

'Indeed, Monsieur.'

'Yes. I think, Luigi, that *tonight of all nights*, I must have my wits about me! *Something* is going to happen, Luigi, and I am not at all sure what it is.'

'Anything I can do. Monsieur –'

Poirot made a sign. Luigi slipped discreetly away. Stephen Carter was returning to the table.

'We are still deserted, Mr Carter,' said Poirot.

'Oh – er – quite,' said the other.

'You know Mr Barton Russell well?'

'Yes, known him a good while.'

'His sister-in-law, little Miss Weatherby, is very charming.'

'Yes, pretty girl.'

'You know her well, too?'

'Quite.'

'Oh, quite, quite,' said Poirot.

Carter stared at him.

The music stopped and the others returned.

Barton Russell said to a waiter:

'Another bottle of champagne – quickly.'

Then he raised his glass.

'See here, folks. I'm going to ask you to drink a toast. To tell you the truth, there's an idea back of this little party tonight. As you know, I'd ordered a table for six. There were only five of us. That gave us an empty place. Then, by a very strange coincidence, M. Hercule Poirot happened to pass by and I asked him to join our party.

'You don't know yet what an apt coincidence that was. You see that empty seat tonight represents a lady – the lady in whose memory this party is being given. This party, ladies and gentlemen, is being held in memory of my dear wife – Iris – who died exactly four years ago on this very date!'

There was a startled movement round the table. Barton Russell, his face quietly impassive, raised his glass.

'I'll ask you to drink to her memory. *Iris!*'

'Iris?' said Poirot sharply.

He looked at the flowers. Barton Russell caught his glance and gently nodded his head.

There were little murmurs round the table.

'Iris – Iris . . .'

Everyone looked startled and uncomfortable.

Barton Russell went on, speaking with his slow

monotonous American intonation, each word coming out weightily.

'It may seem odd to you all that I should celebrate the anniversary of a death in this way – by a supper party in a fashionable restaurant. But I have a reason – yes, I have a reason. For M. Poirot's benefit, I'll explain.'

He turned his head towards Poirot.

'Four years ago tonight, M. Poirot, there was a supper party held in New York. At it were my wife and myself, Mr Stephen Carter, who was attached to the Embassy in Washington, Mr Anthony Chapell, who had been a guest in our house for some weeks, and Señora Valdez, who was at that time enchanting New York City with her dancing. Little Pauline here –' he patted her shoulder '– was only sixteen but she came to the supper party as a special treat. You remember, Pauline?'

'I remember – yes.' Her voice shook a little.

'M. Poirot, on that night a tragedy happened. There was a roll of drums and the cabaret started. The lights went down – all but a spotlight in the middle of the floor. When the lights went up again, M. Poirot, my wife was seen to have fallen forward on the table. She was dead – stone dead. There was potassium cyanide found in the dregs of her wine glass, and the remains of the packet was discovered in her handbag.'

'She had committed suicide?' said Poirot.

'That was the accepted verdict . . . It broke me up,

M. Poirot. There was, perhaps, a possible reason for such an action – the police thought so. I accepted their decision.'

He pounded suddenly on the table.

'But I was not satisfied . . . No, for four years I've been thinking and brooding – and I'm not satisfied: I don't believe Iris killed herself. I believe, M. Poirot, that she was murdered – by one of those people at the table.'

'Look here, sir –'

Tony Chapell half sprung to his feet.

'Be quiet, Tony,' said Russell. 'I haven't finished. One of them did it – I'm sure of that now. Someone who, under cover of the darkness, slipped the half emptied packet of cyanide into her handbag. I think I know which of them it was. I mean to know the truth –'

Lola's voice rose sharply.

'You are mad – crazee – who would have harmed her? No, you are mad. Me, I will not stay –'

She broke off. There was a roll of drums.

Barton Russell said:

'The cabaret. Afterwards we will go on with this. Stay where you are, all of you. I've got to go and speak to the dance band. Little arrangement I've made with them.'

He got up and left the table.

'Extraordinary business,' commented Carter. 'Man's mad.'

'He ees crazee, yes,' said Lola.

The lights were lowered.

'For two pins I'd clear out,' said Tony.

'No!' Pauline spoke sharply. Then she murmured, 'Oh, dear – oh, dear –'

'What is it, Mademoiselle?' murmured Poirot.

She answered almost in a whisper.

'It's horrible! It's just like it was that night –'

'Sh! Sh!' said several people.

Poirot lowered his voice.

'A little word in your ear.' He whispered, then patted her shoulder. 'All will be well,' he assured her.

'My God, listen,' cried Lola.

'What is it, Señora?'

'*It's the same tune* – the same song that they played that night in New York. Barton Russell must have fixed it. I don't like this.'

'Courage – courage –'

There was a fresh hush.

A girl walked out into the middle of the floor, a coal black girl with rolling eyeballs and white glistening teeth. She began to sing in a deep hoarse voice – a voice that was curiously moving.

I've forgotten you
I never think of you
The way you walked

The way you talked
The things you used to say
I've forgotten you
I never think of you
I couldn't say
For sure today
Whether your eyes were blue or grey
I've forgotten you
I never think of you.

I'm through
Thinking of you
I tell you I'm through
Thinking of you . . .
You . . . you . . . you . . .

The sobbing tune, the deep golden Negro voice had a powerful effect. It hypnotized – cast a spell. Even the waiters felt it. The whole room stared at her, hypnotized by the thick cloying emotion she distilled.

A waiter passed softly round the table filling up glasses, murmuring 'champagne' in an undertone but all attention was on the one glowing spot of light – the black woman whose ancestors came from Africa, singing in her deep voice:

I've forgotten you
I never think of you

Oh, what a lie
I shall think of you, think of you, think of you

till I die . . .

The applause broke out frenziedly. The lights went up. Barton Russell came back and slipped into his seat.

'She's great, that girl –' cried Tony.

But his words were cut short by a low cry from Lola.

'*Look – look . . .*'

And then they all saw. Pauline Weatherby dropped forward onto the table.

Lola cried:

'She's dead – just like Iris – like Iris in New York.'

Poirot sprang from his seat, signing to the others to keep back. He bent over the huddled form, very gently lifted a limp hand and felt for a pulse.

His face was white and stern. The others watched him. They were paralysed, held in a trance.

Slowly, Poirot nodded his head.

'Yes, she is dead – *la pauvre petite.* And I sitting by her! Ah! but this time the murderer shall not escape.'

Barton Russell, his face grey, muttered:

'Just like Iris . . . She saw something – Pauline saw something that night – Only she wasn't sure – she told me she wasn't sure . . . We must get the police . . . Oh, God, little Pauline.'

Poirot said:

'Where is her glass?' He raised it to his nose. 'Yes, I can smell the cyanide. A smell of bitter almonds . . . the same method, the same poison . . .'

He picked up her handbag.

'Let us look in her handbag.'

Barton Russell cried out:

'You don't believe this is suicide, too? Not on your life.'

'Wait,' Poirot commanded. 'No, there is nothing here. The lights went up, you see, too quickly, the murderer had not time. Therefore, the poison is still on him.'

'Or her,' said Carter.

He was looking at Lola Valdez.

She spat out:

'What do you mean – what do you say? That I killed her – eet is not true – not true – why should I do such a thing!'

'You had rather a fancy for Barton Russell yourself in New York. That's the gossip I heard. Argentine beauties are notoriously jealous.'

'That ees a pack of lies. And I do not come from the Argentine. I come from Peru. Ah – I spit upon you. I –' She lapsed into Spanish.

'I demand silence,' cried Poirot. 'It is for me to speak.'

Barton Russell said heavily:

'Everyone must be searched.'

Poirot said calmly.

'*Non, non*, it is not necessary.'

'What d'you mean, not necessary?'

'I, Hercule Poirot, know. I see with the eyes of the mind. And I will speak! M. Carter, *will you show us the packet in your breast pocket?*'

'There's nothing in my pocket. What the hell –'

'Tony, my good friend, if you will be so obliging.'

Carter cried out:

'Damn you –'

Tony flipped the packet neatly out before Carter could defend himself.

'There you are, M. Poirot, just as you said!'

'IT'S A DAMNED LIE,' cried Carter.

Poirot picked up the packet, read the label.

'Cyanide potassium. The case is complete.'

Barton Russell's voice came thickly.

'Carter! I always thought so. Iris was in love with you. She wanted to go away with you. You didn't want a scandal for the sake of your precious career so you poisoned her. You'll hang for this, you dirty dog.'

'Silence!' Poirot's voice rang out, firm and authoritative. 'This is not finished yet. I, Hercule Poirot, have something to say. My friend here, Tony Chapell, he says to me when I arrive, that I have come in search of crime. That, it is partly true. There *was* crime in my mind – but it was to prevent a crime that I came. And I have prevented it. The murderer, he planned well – but Hercule Poirot he was one move ahead. He had to think fast, and to whisper quickly in Mademoiselle's ear when the lights went down. She is very quick and clever, Mademoiselle Pauline, she played her part well. Mademoiselle, will you be so kind as to show us that you are not dead after all?'

Pauline sat up. She gave an unsteady laugh.

'Resurrection of Pauline,' she said.

'Pauline – darling.'

'Tony!'

'My sweet!'

'Angel.'

Barton Russell gasped.

'I – I don't understand . . .'

'I will help you to understand, Mr Barton Russell. Your plan has miscarried.'

'My plan?'

'Yes, your plan. Who was the only man who had an *alibi* during the darkness. The man who left the table – you, Mr Barton Russell. But you returned to it under cover of the darkness, circling round it, with a champagne bottle, filling up glasses, putting cyanide in

Pauline's glass and dropping the half empty packet in Carter's pocket as you bent over him to remove a glass. Oh, yes, it is easy to play the part of a waiter in darkness when the attention of everyone is elsewhere. That was the real reason for your party tonight. The safest place to commit a murder is in the middle of a crowd.'

'What the – why the hell should I want to kill Pauline?'

'It might be, perhaps, a question of money. Your wife left you guardian to her sister. You mentioned that fact tonight. Pauline is twenty. At twenty-one or on her marriage you would have to render an account of your stewardship. I suggest that you could not do that. You have speculated with it. I do not know, Mr Barton Russell, whether you killed your wife in the same way, or whether her suicide suggested the idea of this crime to you, but I do know that tonight you have been guilty of attempted murder. It rests with Miss Pauline whether you are prosecuted for that.'

'No,' said Pauline. 'He can get out of my sight and out of this country. I don't want a scandal.'

'You had better go quickly, Mr Barton Russell, and I advise you to be careful in future.'

Barton Russell got up, his face working.

'To hell with you, you interfering little Belgian jack-anapes.'

He strode out angrily.

Pauline sighed.

'M. Poirot, you've been wonderful . . .'

'You, Mademoiselle, you have been the marvellous one. To pour away the champagne, to act the dead body so prettily.'

'Ugh,' she shivered, 'you give me the creeps.'

He said gently:

'It was you who telephoned me, was it not?'

'Yes.'

'Why?'

'I don't know. I was worried and – frightened without knowing quite why I was frightened. Barton told me he was having this party to commemorate Iris' death. I realized he had some scheme on – but he wouldn't tell me what it was. He looked so – so queer and so excited that I felt something terrible might happen – only, of course, I never dreamed that he meant to – to get rid of *me*.'

'And so, Mademoiselle?'

'I'd heard people talking about you. I thought if I could only get you here perhaps it would stop anything happening. I thought that being a – a foreigner – if I rang up and pretended to be in danger and – and made it sound mysterious –'

'You thought the melodrama, it would attract me? That is what puzzled me. The message itself – definitely it was what you call "bogus" – it did not ring true. But the fear in the voice – that was real. Then I came – and you denied very categorically having sent me a message.'

'I had to. Besides, I didn't want you to know it was me.'

'Ah, but I was fairly sure of that! Not at first. But I soon realized that the only two people who could know about the yellow irises on the table were you or Mr Barton Russell.'

Pauline nodded.

'I heard him ordering them to be put on the table,' she explained. 'That, and his ordering a table for six when I knew only five were coming, made me suspect –' She stopped, biting her lip.

'What did you suspect, Mademoiselle?'

She said slowly:

'I was afraid – of something happening – to Mr Carter.'

Stephen Carter cleared his throat. Unhurriedly but quite decisively he rose from the table.

'Er – h'm – I have to – er – thank you, Mr Poirot. I owe you a great deal. You'll excuse me, I'm sure, if I leave you. Tonight's happenings have been – rather upsetting.'

Looking after his retreating figure, Pauline said violently:

'I hate him. I've always thought it was – because of

him that Iris killed herself. Or perhaps – Barton killed her. Oh, it's all so hateful . . .'

Poirot said gently:

'Forget, Mademoiselle . . . forget . . . Let the past go . . . Think only of the present . . .'

Pauline murmured, 'Yes – you're right . . .'

Poirot turned to Lola Valdez.

'Señora, as the evening advances I become more brave. If you would dance with me now –'

'Oh, yes, indeed. You are – you are ze cat's whiskers, M. Poirot. I inseest on dancing with you.'

'You are too kind, Señora.'

Tony and Pauline were left. They leant towards each other across the table.

'Darling Pauline.'

'Oh, Tony, I've been such a nasty spiteful spitfiring little cat to you all day. Can you ever forgive me?'

'Angel! This is Our Tune again. Let's dance.'

They danced off, smiling at each other and humming softly:

There's nothing like Love for making you miserable
There's nothing like Love for making you blue
Depressed
Possessed
Sentimental
Temperamental

There's nothing like Love
For getting you down.

There's nothing like Love for driving you crazy
There's nothing like Love for making you mad
Abusive
Allusive
Suicidal
Homicidal
There's nothing like Love
There's nothing like Love . . .

The Harlequin Tea Set

Mr Satterthwaite clucked twice in vexation. Whether right in his assumption or not, he was more and more convinced that cars nowadays broke down far more frequently than they used to do. The only cars he trusted were old friends who had survived the test of time. They had their little idiosyncrasies, but you knew about those, provided for them, fulfilled their wants before the demand became too acute. But new cars! Full of new gadgets, different kinds of windows, an instrument panel newly and differently arranged, handsome in its glistening wood but being unfamiliar, your groping hand hovered uneasily over fog lights, windscreen wipers, the choke, etcetera. All these things with knobs in a place you didn't expect them. And when your gleaming new purchase failed in performance, your local garage uttered the intensely irritating words: 'Teething troubles. Splendid car, sir, these roadsters Super Superbos. All the latest accessories. But bound to have their teething troubles, you know. Ha, ha.' Just as though a car was a baby.

But Mr Satterthwaite, being now of an advanced age, was strongly of the opinion that a new car ought to be fully adult. Tested, inspected, and its teething troubles already dealt with before it came into its purchaser's possession.

Mr Satterthwaite was on his way to pay a weekend visit to friends in the country. His new car had already, on the way from London, given certain symptoms of discomfort, and was now drawn up in a garage waiting for the diagnosis, and how long it would take before he could resume progress towards his destination. His chauffeur was in consultation with a mechanic. Mr Satterthwaite sat, striving for patience. He had assured his hosts, on the telephone the night before, that he would be arriving in good time for tea. He would reach Doverton Kingsbourne, he assured them, well before four o'clock.

He clucked again in irritation and tried to turn his thoughts to something pleasant. It was no good sitting here in a state of acute irritation, frequently consulting his wristwatch, clucking once more and giving, he had to realize, a very good imitation of a hen pleased with its prowess in laying an egg.

Yes. Something pleasant. Yes, now hadn't there been

something – something he had noticed as they were driving along. Not very long ago. Something that he had seen through the window which had pleased and excited him. But before he had had time to think about it, the car's misbehaviour had become more pronounced and a rapid visit to the nearest service station had been inevitable.

What was it that he had seen? On the left – no, on the right. Yes, on the right as they drove slowly through the village street. Next door to a post office. Yes, he was quite sure of that. Next door to a post office because the sight of the post office had given him the idea of telephoning to the Addisons to break the news that he might be slightly late in his arrival. The post office. A village post office. And next to it – yes, definitely, next to it, next door or if not next door the door after. Something that had stirred old memories, and he had wanted – just what was it that he had wanted? Oh dear, it would come to him presently. It was mixed up with a colour. Several colours. Yes, a colour or colours. Or a word. Some definite word that had stirred memories, thoughts, pleasures gone by, excitement, recalling something that had been vivid and alive. Something in which he himself had not only seen but observed. No, he had done more. He had taken part. Taken part in what, and why, and where? All sorts of places. The answer came quickly at the last thought. All sorts of places.

On an island? In Corsica? At Monte Carlo watching the croupier spinning his roulette wheel? A house in the country? All sorts of places. And he had been there, and someone else. Yes, someone else. It all tied up with that. He was getting there at last. If he could just . . . He was interrupted at that moment by the chauffeur coming to the window with the garage mechanic in tow behind him.

'Won't be long now, sir,' the chauffeur assured Mr Satterthwaite cheerfully. 'Matter of ten minutes or so. Not more.'

'Nothing seriously wrong,' said the mechanic, in a low, hoarse, country voice. 'Teething troubles, as you might say.'

Mr Satterthwaite did not cluck this time. He gnashed his own teeth. A phrase he had often read in books and which in old age he seemed to have got into the habit of doing himself, due, perhaps, to the slight looseness of his upper plate. Really, teething trouble! Toothache. Teeth gnashing. False teeth. One's whole life centred, he thought, about teeth.

'Doverton Kingsbourne's only a few miles away,' said the chauffeur, 'and they've a taxi here. You could go on in that, sir, and I'd bring the car along later as soon as it's fixed up.'

'No!' said Mr Satterthwaite.

He said the word explosively and both the chauffeur and the mechanic looked startled. Mr Satterthwaite's eyes were sparkling. His voice was clear and decisive. Memory had come to him.

'I propose,' he said, 'to walk along the road we have just come by. When the car is ready, you will pick me up there. The Harlequin Cafe, I think it is called.'

'It's not very much of a place, sir,' the mechanic advised.

'That is where I shall be,' said Mr Satterthwaite, speaking with a kind of regal autocracy.

He walked off briskly. The two men stared after him.

'Don't know what's got into him,' said the chauffeur. 'Never seen him like that before.'

The village of Kingsbourne Ducis did not live up to the old world grandeur of its name. It was a smallish village consisting of one street. A few houses. Shops that were dotted rather unevenly, sometimes betraying the fact that they were houses which had been turned into shops or that they were shops which now existed as houses without any industrial intentions.

It was not particularly old world or beautiful. It was just simple and rather unobtrusive. Perhaps that was why, thought Mr Satterthwaite, that a dash of brilliant colour had caught his eye. Ah, here he was at the post office. The post office was a simply functioning post office with a pillar box outside, a display of some newspapers and some postcards, and surely, next to it, yes there was the sign up above. The Harlequin Cafe. A sudden qualm struck Mr Satterthwaite. Really, he was getting too old. He had fancies. Why should that one word stir his heart? *The Harlequin Cafe.*

The mechanic at the service station had been quite right. It did not look like a place in which one would really be tempted to have a meal. A snack perhaps. A morning coffee. Then why? But he suddenly realized why. Because the cafe, or perhaps one could better put it as the house that sheltered the cafe was in two portions. One side of it had small tables with chairs round them arranged ready for patrons who came here to eat. But the other side was a shop. A shop that sold china. It was not an antique shop. It had no little shelves of glass vases or mugs. It was a shop that sold modern goods, and the show window that gave on the street was at the present moment housing every shade of the rainbow. A tea set of largish cups and saucers, each one of a different colour. Blue, red, yellow, green, pink, purple. Really, Mr Satterthwaite thought, a wonderful show of colour. No wonder it had struck his eye as the car had passed slowly beside the pavement, looking ahead for any sign of a garage or a service station. It was labelled with a large card as 'A Harlequin Tea Set'.

It was the word 'harlequin' of course which had remained fixed in Mr Satterthwaite's mind, although just far enough back in his mind so that it had been difficult to recall it. The gay colours. The harlequin colours. And he had thought, wondered, had the absurd but exciting idea that in some way here was a call to him. To him specially. Here, perhaps, eating a meal or purchasing cups and saucers might be his own old friend, Mr Harley Quin. How many years was it since he had last seen Mr Quin? A large number of years. Was it the day he had seen Mr Quin walking away from him down a country lane, Lovers' Lane they had called it? He had always expected to see Mr Quin again, once a year at least. Possibly twice a year. But no. That had not happened.

And so today he had had the wonderful and surprising idea that here, in the village of Kingsbourne Ducis, he might once again find Mr Harley Quin.

'Absurd of me,' said Mr Satterthwaite, 'quite absurd of me. Really, the ideas one has as one gets old!'

He had missed Mr Quin. Missed something that had been one of the most exciting things in the late years of his life. Someone who might turn up anywhere and who, if he did turn up, was always an announcement that something was going to happen. Something that was going to happen to him. No, that was not quite right. Not *to* him, but through him. That was the exciting part. Just from the words that Mr Quin might utter. Words. Things he might show him, ideas would come to Mr Satterthwaite. He would see things, he would imagine things, he would find out things. He would deal with something that needed to be dealt with. And opposite him would sit Mr Quin, perhaps smiling approval. Something that Mr Quin said would start the flow of ideas, the active person would be he himself. He – Mr Satterthwaite. The man with so many old friends. A man among whose friends had been duchesses, an occasional bishop, people that counted. Especially, he had to admit, people who had counted in the social world. Because, after all, Mr Satterthwaite had always been a snob. He had liked duchesses, he had liked knowing old families, families who had represented the landed gentry of England for several generations. And he had had, too, an interest in young people not necessarily socially important. Young people who were in trouble, who were in love, who were unhappy, who needed help. Because of Mr Quin, Mr Satterthwaite was enabled to give help.

And now, like an idiot, he was looking into an unprepossessing village cafe and a shop for modern china and tea sets and casseroles no doubt.

'All the same,' said Mr Satterthwaite to himself, 'I must go in. Now I've been foolish enough to walk back here, I must go in just – well, just in case. They'll be longer, I expect, doing the car than they say. It will be more than ten minutes. Just in case there was anything interesting inside.'

He looked once more at the window full of china. He appreciated suddenly that it was good china. Well made. A good modern product. He looked back into the past, remembering. The Duchess of Leith, he remembered. What a wonderful old lady she had been. How kind she had been to her maid on the occasion of a very rough sea voyage to the island of Corsica. She had ministered to her with the kindliness of a ministering angel and only on the next day had she resumed her autocratic, bullying manner which the domestics of those days had seemed able to stand quite easily without any sign of rebellion.

Maria. Yes, that's what the Duchess's name had been. Dear old Maria Leith. Ah well. She had died some years ago. But she had had a harlequin breakfast set, he remembered. Yes. Big round cups in different colours. Black. Yellow, red and a particularly pernicious shade of puce. Puce, he thought, must have been a favourite colour of hers. She had had a Rockingham tea set, he remembered, in which the predominating colour had been puce decorated with gold.

'Ah,' sighed Mr Satterthwaite, 'those were the days. Well, I suppose I'd better go in. Perhaps order a cup of coffee or something. It will be very full of milk, I expect, and possibly already sweetened. But still, one has to pass the time.'

He went in. The cafe side was practically empty. It was early, Mr Satterthwaite supposed, for people to want cups of tea. And anyway, very few people did want cups of tea nowadays. Except, that is, occasionally elderly people in their own homes. There was a young couple in the far window and two women gossiping at a table against the back wall.

'I said to her,' one of them was saying, 'I said you can't do that sort of thing. No, it's not the sort of thing that I'll put up with, and I said the same to Henry and he agreed with me.'

It shot through Mr Satterthwaite's mind that Henry must have rather a hard life and that no doubt he had found it always wise to agree, whatever the proposition put up to him might be. A most unattractive woman with a most unattractive friend. He turned his attention to the other side of the building, murmuring, 'May I just look round?'

There was quite a pleasant woman in charge and she said 'Oh yes, sir. We've got a good stock at present.'

Mr Satterthwaite looked at the coloured cups, picked up one or two of them, examined the milk jug, picked up a china zebra and considered it, examined some ashtrays of a fairly pleasing pattern. He heard chairs being pushed back and turning his head, noted that the two middle-aged women still discussing former grievances had paid their bill and were now leaving the shop. As they went out of the door, a tall man in a dark suit came in. He sat down at the table which they had just vacated. His back was to Mr Satterthwaite, who thought that he had an attractive back. Lean, strong, well-muscled but rather dark and sinister-looking because there was very little light in the shop. Mr Satterthwaite looked back again at the ashtrays. 'I might buy an ashtray so as not to cause a disappointment to the shop owner,' he thought. As he did so, the sun came out suddenly.

He had not realized that the shop had looked dim because of the lack of sunshine. The sun must have been under a cloud for some time. It had clouded over, he remembered, at about the time they had got to the service station. But now there was this sudden burst of sunlight. It caught up the colours of the china and through a coloured glass window of somewhat ecclesiastical pattern which must, Mr Satterthwaite thought, have been left over in the original Victorian house. The sun came through the window and lit up the dingy cafe. In some curious way it lit up the back of the man who had just sat down there. Instead of a dark black silhouette, there was now a festoon of colours. Red and blue and yellow. And suddenly Mr Satterthwaite realized that he was looking at exactly what he had hoped to find. His intuition had not played him false. He knew who it was who had just come in and sat down there. He knew so well that he had no need to wait until he could look at the face. He turned his back on the china, went back into the cafe, round the corner of the round table and sat down opposite the man who had just come in.

'Mr Quin,' said Mr Satterthwaite. 'I knew somehow it was going to be you.'

Mr Quin smiled.

'You always know so many things,' he said.

'It's a long time since I've seen you,' said Mr Satterthwaite.

'Does time matter?' said Mr Quin.

'Perhaps not. You may be right. Perhaps not.'

'May I offer you some refreshment?'

'Is there any refreshment to be had?' said Mr Satterthwaite doubtfully. 'I suppose you must have come in for that purpose.'

'One is never quite sure of one's purpose, is one?' said Mr Quin.

'I am so pleased to see you again,' said Mr Satterthwaite. 'I'd almost forgotten, you know. I mean forgotten the way you talk, the things you say. The things you make me think of, the things you make me do.'

'I – make you do? You are so wrong. You have always known yourself just what you wanted to do and why you want to do them and why you know so well that they have to be done.'

'I only feel that when you are here.'

'Oh no,' said Mr Quin lightly. 'I have nothing to do with it. I am just – as I've often told you – I am just passing by. That is all.'

'Today you are passing by through Kingsbourne Ducis.'

'And you are not passing by. You are going to a definite place. Am I right?'

'I'm going to see a very old friend. A friend I have not seen for a good many years. He's old now. Somewhat crippled. He has had one stroke. He has recovered from it quite well, but one never knows.'

'Does he live by himself?'

'Not now, I am glad to say. His family have come back from abroad, what is left of his family that is. They have been living with him now for some months. I am glad to be able to come and see them again all together. Those, that's to say, that I have seen before, and those that I have not seen.'

'You mean children?'

'Children and grandchildren.' Mr Satterthwaite sighed. Just for a moment he was sad that he had had no children and no grandchildren and no great-grandchildren himself. He did not usually regret it at all.

'They have some special Turkish coffee here,' said

Mr Quin. 'Really good of its kind. Everything else is, as you have guessed, rather unpalatable. But one can always have a cup of Turkish coffee, can one not? Let us have one because I suppose you will soon have to get on with your pilgrimage, or whatever it is.'

In the doorway came a small black dog. He came and sat down by the table and looked up at Mr Quin.

'Your dog?' said Mr Satterthwaite.

'Yes. Let me introduce you to Hermes.' He stroked the black dog's head. 'Coffee,' he said. 'Tell Ali.'

The black dog walked from the table through a door at the back of the shop. They heard him give a short, incisive bark. Presently he reappeared and with him came a young man with a very dark complexion, wearing an emerald green pullover.

'Coffee, Ali,' said Mr Quin. 'Two coffees.'

'Turkish coffee. That's right, isn't it, sir?' He smiled and disappeared.

The dog sat down again.

'Tell me,' said Mr Satterthwaite, 'tell me where you've been and what you have been doing and why I have not seen you for so long.'

'I have just told you that time really means nothing. It is clear in my mind and I think it is clear in yours the occasion when we last met.'

'A very tragic occasion,' said Mr Satterthwaite. 'I do not really like to think of it.'

'Because of death? But death is not always a tragedy. I have told you that before.'

'No,' said Mr Satterthwaite, 'perhaps that death – the one we are both thinking of – was not a tragedy. But all the same . . .'

'But all the same it is life that really matters. You are quite right, of course,' said Mr Quin. 'Quite right. It is life that matters. We do not want someone young, someone who is happy, or could be happy, to die. Neither of us want that, do we. That is the reason why we must always save a life when the command comes.'

'Have you got a command for me?'

'Me – command for you?' Harley Quin's long, sad face brightened into its peculiarly charming smile. 'I have no commands for *you*, Mr Satterthwaite. I have never had commands. You yourself know things, see things, know what to do, do them. It has nothing to do with me.'

'Oh yes, it has,' said Mr Satterthwaite. 'You're not going to change my mind on that point. But tell me. Where have you been during what it is too short to call time?'

'Well, I have been here and there. In different countries, different climates, different adventures. But mostly, as usual, just passing by. I think it is more for you to tell me not only what you have been doing but what you are going to do now. More about where you are going. Who you are going to meet. Your friends, what they are like.'

'Of course I will tell you. I should enjoy telling you because I have been wondering, thinking you know about these friends I am going to. When you have not seen a family for a long time, when you have not been closely connected with them for many years, it is always a nervous moment when you are going to resume old friendships and old ties.'

'You are so right,' said Mr Quin.

The Turkish coffee was brought in little cups of oriental pattern. Ali placed them with a smile and departed. Mr Satterthwaite sipped approvingly.

'As sweet as love, as black as night and as hot as hell. That is the old Arab phrase, isn't it?'

Harley smiled over his shoulder and nodded.

'Yes,' said Mr Satterthwaite, 'I must tell you where I am going though what I am doing hardly matters. I am going to renew old friendships, to make acquaintance with the younger generation. Tom Addison, as I have said, is a very old friend of mine. We did many things together in our young days. Then, as often happens, life parted us. He was in the Diplomatic Service, went abroad for several foreign posts in turn. Sometimes I went and stayed with him, sometimes I saw him when he was home in England. One of his early posts was in Spain. He married a Spanish girl, a very beautiful, dark girl called Pilar. He loved her very much.'

'They had children?'

'Two daughters. A fair-haired baby like her father, called Lily, and a second daughter, Maria, who took after her Spanish mother. I was Lily's godfather. Naturally, I did not see either of the children very often. Two or three times a year either I gave a party for Lily or went to see her at her school. She was a sweet and lovely person. Very devoted to her father and he was very devoted to her. But in between these meetings, these revivals of friendship, we went through some difficult times. You will know about it as well as I do. I and my contemporaries had difficulties in meeting through the war years. Lily married a pilot in the Air Force. A fighter pilot. Until the other day I had even forgotten his name. Simon Gilliatt. Squadron Leader Gilliatt.'

'He was killed in the war?'

'No, no. No. He came through safely. After the war he resigned from the Air Force and he and Lily went out to Kenya as so many did. They settled there and they lived very happily. They had a son, a little boy called Roland. Later when he was at school in England I saw him once or twice. The last time, I think, was when he was twelve years old. A nice boy. He had red hair like his father. I've not seen him since so I am looking forward to seeing him today. He is twenty-three – twenty-four now. Time goes on so.'

'Is he married?'

'No. Well, not yet.'

'Ah. Prospects of marriage?'

'Well, I wondered from something Tom Addison said in his letter. There is a girl cousin. The younger daughter Maria married the local doctor. I never knew her very well. It was rather sad. She died in childbirth. Her little girl was called Inez, a family name chosen by her Spanish grandmother. As it happens I have only seen Inez once since she grew up. A dark, Spanish type very much like her grandmother. But I am boring you with all this.'

'No. I want to hear it. It is very interesting to me.'

'I wonder why,' said Mr Satterthwaite.

He looked at Mr Quin with that slight air of suspicion which sometimes came to him.

'You want to know all about this family. Why?'

'So that I can picture it, perhaps, in my mind.'

'Well, this house I am going to, Doverton Kingsbourne it is called. It is quite a beautiful old house. Not so spectacular as to invite tourists or to be open to visitors on special days. Just a quiet country house to live in by an Englishman who has served his country and comes back to enjoy a mellow life when the age of retirement comes. Tom was always fond of country life. He enjoyed fishing. He was a good shot and we had very happy days together in his family home of his boyhood. I spent many of my own holidays as a boy at Doverton Kingsbourne. And all through my life I have had that image in my mind. No place like Doverton Kingsbourne. No other house to touch it. Every time I drove near it I would make a detour perhaps and just pass to see the view through a gap in the trees of the long lane that runs in front of the house, glimpses of the river where we used to fish, and of the house itself. And I would remember all the things that Tom and I did together. He has been a man of action. A man who has done things. And I – I have just been an old bachelor.'

'You have been more than that,' said Mr Quin. 'You have been a man who made friends, who had many friends and who has served his friends well.'

'Well, if I can think that. Perhaps you are being too kind.'

'Not at all. You are very good company besides. The stories you can tell, the things you've seen, the places you have visited. The curious things that have happened in your life. You could write a whole book on them,' said Mr Quin.

'I should make you the main character in it if I did.'

'No, you would not,' said Mr Quin. 'I am the

one who passes by. That is all. But go on. Tell me more.'

'Well, this is just a family chronicle that I'm telling you. As I say, there were long periods, years of time when I did not see any of them. But they have been always my old friends. I saw Tom and Pilar until the time when Pilar died – she died rather young, unfortunately – Lily, my godchild, Inez, the quiet doctor's daughter who lives in the village with her father . . .'

'How old is the daughter?'

'Inez is nineteen or twenty, I think. I shall be glad to make friends with her.'

'So it is on the whole a happy chronicle?'

'Not entirely. Lily, my godchild – the one who went to Kenya with her husband – was killed there in an automobile accident. She was killed outright, leaving behind her a baby of barely a year old, little Roland. Simon, her husband, was quite broken-hearted. They were an unusually happy couple. However, the best thing happened to him that could happen, I suppose. He married again, a young widow who was the widow of a Squadron Leader, a friend of his and who also had been left with a baby the same age. Little Timothy and little Roland had only two or three months in age between them. Simon's marriage, I believe, has been quite happy though I've not seen them, of course, because they continued to live in Kenya. The boys were brought up like brothers. They went to the same school in England and spent their holidays usually in Kenya. I have not seen them, of course, for many years. Well, you know what has happened in Kenya. Some people have managed to stay on. Some people, friends of mine, have gone to Western Australia and have settled again happily there with their families. Some have come home to this country.

'Simon Gilliatt and his wife and their two children left Kenya. It was not the same to them and so they came home and accepted the invitation that has always been given them and renewed every year by old Tom Addison. They have come, his son-in-law, his son-in-law's second wife and the two children, now grown up boys, or rather, young men. They have come to live as a family there and they are happy. Tom's other grandchild, Inez Horton, as I told you, lives in the village with her father, the doctor, and she spends a good deal of her time, I gather, at Doverton Kingsbourne with Tom Addison who is very devoted to his grand-daughter. They sound all very happy together there. He has urged me several times to come there and see. Meet them all again. And so I accepted the invitation. Just for a weekend. It will be sad in some ways to see dear old Tom again, somewhat crippled, with perhaps not a very long expectation of life but still cheerful and gay, as far as I can make out. And to see also the old house again. Doverton Kingsbourne. Tied up with all my boyish memories. When one has not lived a very eventful life, when nothing has happened to one personally, and that is true of me, the things that remain with you are the friends, the houses and the things you did as a child and a boy and a young man. There is only one thing that worries me.'

'You should not be worried. What is it that worries you?'

'That I might be – disappointed. The house one remembers, one has dreams of, when one might come to see it again it would not be as you remembered it or dreamt it. A new wing would have been added, the garden would have been altered, all sorts of things can have happened to it. It is a very long time, really, since I have been there.'

'I think your memories will go with you,' said Mr Quin. 'I am glad you are going there.'

'I have an idea,' said Mr Satterthwaite. 'Come with me. Come with me on this visit. You need not fear that you'll not be welcome. Dear Tom Addison is the most hospitable fellow in the world. Any friend of mine would immediately be a friend of his. Come with me. You must. I insist.'

Making an impulsive gesture, Mr Satterthwaite nearly

knocked his coffee cup off the table. He caught it just in time.

At that moment the shop door was pushed open, ringing its old-fashioned bell as it did so. A middle-aged woman came in. She was slightly out of breath and looked somewhat hot. She was good-looking still with a head of auburn hair only just touched here and there with grey. She had that clear ivory-coloured skin that so often goes with reddish hair and blue eyes, and she had kept her figure well. The newcomer swept a quick glance round the cafe and turned immediately into the china shop.

'Oh!' she exclaimed, 'you've still got some of the Harlequin cups.'

'Yes, Mrs Gilliatt, we had a new stock arrived in yesterday.'

'Oh, I'm so pleased. I really have been very worried. I rushed down here. I took one of the boys' motor bikes. They'd gone off somewhere and I couldn't find either of them. But I really had to do something. There was an unfortunate accident this morning with some of the cups and we've got people arriving for tea and a party this afternoon. So if you can give me a blue and a green and perhaps I'd better have another red one as well in case. That's the worst of these different coloured cups, isn't it?'

'Well, I know they do say as it's a disadvantage

and you can't always replace the particular colour you want.'

Mr Satterthwaite's head had gone over his shoulder now and he was looking with some interest at what was going on. Mrs Gilliatt, the shop woman had said. But of course. He realized it now. This must be – he rose from his seat, half hesitating, and then took a step or two into the shop.

'Excuse me,' he said, 'but are you – are you Mrs Gilliatt from Doverton Kingsbourne?'

'Oh yes. I am Beryl Gilliatt. Do you – I mean . . . ?'

She looked at him, wrinkling her brows a little. An attractive woman, Mr Satterthwaite thought. Rather a hard face, perhaps, but competent. So this was Simon Gilliatt's second wife. She hadn't got the beauty of Lily, but she seemed an attractive woman, pleasant and efficient. Suddenly a smile came to Mrs Gilliatt's face.

'I do believe . . . yes, of course. My father-in-law, Tom, has got a photograph of you and you must be the guest we are expecting this afternoon. You must be Mr Satterthwaite.'

'Exactly,' said Mr Satterthwaite. 'That is who I am. But I shall have to apologize very much for being so much later in arriving than I said. But unfortunately my car has had a breakdown. It's in the garage now being attended to.'

'Oh, how miserable for you. But what a shame. But

it's not tea time yet. Don't worry. We've put it off anyway. As you probably heard, I ran down to replace a few cups which unfortunately got swept off a table this morning. Whenever one has anyone to lunch or tea or dinner, something like that always happens.'

'There you are, Mrs Gilliatt,' said the woman in the shop. 'I'll wrap them up in here. Shall I put them in a box for you?'

'No, if you'll just put some paper around them and put them in this shopping bag of mine, they'll be quite all right that way.'

'If you are returning to Doverton Kingsbourne,' said Mr Satterthwaite, 'I could give you a lift in my car. It will be arriving from the garage any moment now.'

'That's very kind of you. I wish really I could accept. But I've simply got to take the motorbike back. The boys will be miserable without it. They're going somewhere this evening.'

'Let me introduce you,' said Mr Satterthwaite. He turned towards Mr Quin, who had risen to his feet and was now standing quite near. 'This is an old friend of mine, Mr Harley Quin, whom I have just happened to run across here. I've been trying to persuade him to come along to Doverton Kingsbourne. Would it be possible, do you think, for Tom to put up yet another guest for tonight?'

'Oh, I'm sure it would be quite all right,' said Beryl

Gilliatt. 'I'm sure he'd be delighted to see another friend of yours. Perhaps it's a friend of his as well.'

'No,' said Mr Quin, 'I've never met Mr Addison though I've often heard my friend, Mr Satterthwaite, speak of him.'

'Well then, do let Mr Satterthwaite bring you. We should be delighted.'

'I am very sorry,' said Mr Quin. 'Unfortunately, I have another engagement. Indeed –' he looked at his watch '– I must start for it immediately. I am late already, which is what comes of meeting old friends.'

'Here you are, Mrs Gilliatt,' said the saleswoman. 'It'll be quite all right, I think, in your bag.'

Beryl Gilliatt put the parcel carefully into the bag she was carrying, then said to Mr Satterthwaite:

'Well, see you presently. Tea isn't until quarter past five, so don't worry. I'm so pleased to meet you at last, having heard so much about you always both from Simon and from my father-in-law.'

She said a hurried goodbye to Mr Quin and went out of the shop.

'Bit of a hurry she's in, isn't she?' said the shop woman, 'but she's always like that. Gets through a lot in a day, I'd say.'

The sound of the bicycle outside was heard as it revved up.

'Quite a character, isn't she?' said Mr Satterthwaite.

'It would seem so,' said Mr Quin.

'And I really can't persuade you?'

'I'm only passing by,' said Mr Quin.

'And when shall I see you again? I wonder now.'

'Oh, it will not be very long,' said Mr Quin. 'I think you will recognize me when you do see me.'

'Have you nothing more – nothing more to tell me? Nothing more to explain?'

'To explain what?'

'To explain why I have met you here.'

'You are a man of considerable knowledge,' said Mr Quin. 'One word might mean something to you. I think it would and it might come in useful.'

'What word?'

'Daltonism,' said Mr Quin. He smiled.

'I don't think –' Mr Satterthwaite frowned for a moment. 'Yes. Yes, I do know only just for the moment I can't remember . . .'

'Goodbye for the present,' said Mr Quin. 'Here is your car.'

At that moment the car was indeed pulling up by the post office door. Mr Satterthwaite went out to it. He was anxious not to waste more time and keep his hosts waiting longer than need be. But he was sad all the same at saying goodbye to his friend.

'There is nothing I can do for you?' he said, and his tone was almost wistful.

'Nothing you can do for *me.*'

'For someone else?'

'I think so. Very likely.'

'I hope I know what you mean.'

'I have the utmost faith in you,' said Mr Quin. 'You always know things. You are very quick to observe and to know the meaning of things. You have not changed, I assure you.'

His hand rested for a moment on Mr Satterthwaite's shoulder, then he walked out and proceeded briskly down the village street in the opposite direction to Doverton Kingsbourne. Mr Satterthwaite got into his car.

'I hope we shan't have any more trouble,' he said.

His chauffeur reassured him.

'It's no distance from here, sir. Three or four miles at most, and she's running beautifully now.'

He ran the car a little way along the street and turned where the road widened so as to return the way he had just come. He said again,

'Only three or four miles.'

Mr Satterthwaite said again, 'Daltonism.' It still didn't mean anything to him, but yet he felt it should. It was a word he'd heard used before.

'Doverton Kingsbourne,' said Mr Satterthwaite to himself. He said it very softly under his breath. The two words still meant to him what they had always meant. A place of joyous reunion, a place where he couldn't get there too quickly. A place where he was going to enjoy himself, even though so many of those whom he had known would not be there any longer. But Tom would be there. His old friend, Tom, and he thought again of the grass and the lake and the river and the things they had done together as boys.

Tea was set out upon the lawn. Steps led out from the French windows in the drawing room and down to where a big copper beech at one side and a cedar of Lebanon on the other made the setting for the afternoon scene. There were two painted and carved white tables and various garden chairs. Upright ones with coloured cushions and lounging ones where you could lean back and stretch your feet out and sleep, if you wished to do so. Some of them had hoods over them to guard you from the sun.

It was a beautiful early evening and the green of the grass was a soft deep colour. The golden light came through the copper beech and the cedar showed the lines of its beauty against a soft pinkish-golden sky.

Tom Addison was waiting for his guest in a long basket chair, his feet up, Mr Satterthwaite noted with some amusement what he remembered from many other occasions of meeting his host, he had comfortable bedroom slippers suited to his slightly swollen gouty feet, and the shoes were odd ones. One red and one green. Good old Tom, thought Mr Satterthwaite, he hasn't changed. Just the same. And he thought, 'What an idiot I am. Of course I know what that word meant. Why didn't I think of it at once?'

'Thought you were never going to turn up, you old devil,' said Tom Addison.

He was still a handsome old man, a broad face with deep-set twinkling grey eyes, shoulders that were still square and gave him a look of power. Every line in his face seemed a line of good humour and of affectionate welcome. 'He never changes,' thought Mr Satterthwaite.

'Can't get up to greet you,' said Tom Addison. 'Takes two strong men and a stick to get me on my feet. Now, do you know our little crowd, or don't you? You know Simon, of course.'

'Of course I do. It's a good few years since I've seen you, but you haven't changed much.'

Squadron Leader Simon Gilliatt was a lean, handsome man with a mop of red hair.

'Sorry you never came to see us when we were in Kenya,' he said. 'You'd have enjoyed yourself. Lots of things we could have shown you. Ah well, one can't see what the future may bring. I thought I'd lay my bones in that country.'

'We've got a very nice churchyard here,' said Tom Addison. 'Nobody's ruined our church yet by restoring it and we haven't very much new building round about so there's plenty of room in the churchyard still. We haven't had one of these terrible additions of a new intake of graves.'

'What a gloomy conversation you're having,' said Beryl Gilliatt, smiling. 'These are our boys,' she said, 'but you know them already, don't you, Mr Satterthwaite?'

'I don't think I'd have known them now,' said Mr Satterthwaite.

Indeed, the last time he had seen the two boys was on a day when he had taken them out from their prep school. Although there was no relationship between them – they had had different fathers and mothers – yet the boys could have been, and often were, taken for brothers. They were about the same height and they both had red hair. Roland, presumably, having inherited it from his father and Timothy from his auburn-haired mother. There seemed also to be a kind of comradeship between them. Yet really, Mr Satterthwaite thought, they were very different. The difference was clearer now when they were, he supposed, between twenty-two and twenty-five years old. He could see no resemblance in Roland to his grandfather. Nor apart from his red hair did he look like his father.

Mr Satterthwaite had wondered sometimes whether the boy would look like Lily, his dead mother. But there again he could see little resemblance. If anything, Timothy looked more as a son of Lily's might have looked. The fair skin and the high forehead and a delicacy of bone structure. At his elbow, a soft deep voice said,

'I'm Inez. I don't expect you remember me. It was quite a long time ago when I saw you.'

A beautiful girl, Mr Satterthwaite thought at once. A dark type. He cast his mind back a long way to the days when he had come to be best man at Tom Addison's wedding to Pilar. She showed her Spanish blood, he thought, the carriage of her head and the dark aristocratic beauty. Her father, Dr Horton, was standing just behind her. He looked much older than when Mr Satterthwaite had seen him last. A nice man and kindly. A good general practitioner, unambitious but reliable and devoted, Mr Satterthwaite thought, to his daughter. He was obviously immensely proud of her.

Mr Satterthwaite felt an enormous happiness creeping over him. All these people, he thought, although some of them strange to him, it seemed like friends he had already known. The dark beautiful girl, the two red-haired boys, Beryl Gilliatt, fussing over the tea tray, arranging cups and saucers, beckoning to a maid from the house to bring out cakes and plates of sandwiches. A splendid tea. There were chairs that pulled up to the tables so that you could sit comfortably eating all you wanted to eat. The boys settled themselves, inviting Mr Satterthwaite to sit between them.

He was pleased at that. He had already planned in his own mind that it was the boys he wanted to talk to first, to see how much they recalled to him Tom Addison in the old days, and he thought, 'Lily. How I wish Lily could be here now. Here he was, thought Mr Satterthwaite, here he was back in his boyhood. Here where he had come and been welcomed by Tom's father and mother, an aunt or so, too, there had been and a great-uncle and cousins. And now, well, there were not so many in this family, but it *was* a family. Tom in his bedroom slippers, one red, one green, old but still merry and happy. Happy in those who were spread round him. And here was Doverton just, or almost just, as it had been. Not quite so well kept up, perhaps, but the lawn was in good condition. And down there he could see the gleam of the river through the trees and the trees, too. More trees than there had been. And the house needing, perhaps, another coat of paint but not too badly. After all, Tom Addison was a rich man. Well provided for, owning a large quantity of land. A man with simple tastes who spent enough to keep his place up but was not a spendthrift in other ways. He seldom travelled or went abroad nowadays, but he entertained. Not big parties, just friends. Friends who came to stay, friends who usually had some connection going back into the past. A friendly house.

He turned a little in his chair, drawing it away from the table and turning it sideways so that he could see better the view down to the river. Down there was the mill, of course, and beyond the other side there were fields. And in one of the fields, it amused him to see a kind of scarecrow, a dark figure on which birds were settling on the straw. Just for a moment he thought it looked like Mr Harley Quin. Perhaps, thought Mr Satterthwaite, it *is* my friend Mr Quin. It was an absurd idea and yet if someone had piled up the scarecrow and tried to make it look like Mr Quin, it could have had the sort of slender elegance that was foreign to most scarecrows one saw.

'Are you looking at our scarecrow?' said Timothy. 'We've got a name for him, you know. We call him Mister Harley Barley.'

'Do you indeed' said Mr Satterthwaite. 'Dear me, I find that very interesting.'

'Why do you find it interesting?' said Roly, with some curiosity.

'Well, because it rather resembles someone that I know, whose name happens to be Harley. His first name, that is.'

The boys began singing, '*Harley Barley, stands on*

guard, Harley Barley takes things hard. Guards the ricks and guards the hay, Keeps the trespassers away.'

'Cucumber sandwich, Mr Satterthwaite?' said Beryl Gilliatt, 'or do you prefer a home-made pâté one?'

Mr Satterthwaite accepted the home-made pâté. She deposited by his side a puce cup, the same colour as he had admired in the shop. How gay it looked, all that tea set on the table. Yellow, red, blue, green and all the rest of it. He wondered if each one had their favourite colour. Timothy, he noticed, had a red cup, Roland had a yellow one. Beside Timothy's cup was an object Mr Satterthwaite could not at first identify. Then he saw it was a meerschaum pipe. It was years since Mr Satterthwaite had thought of or seen a meerschaum pipe. Roland, noticing what he was looking at, said, 'Tim brought that back from Germany when he went. He's killing himself with cancer smoking his pipe all the time.'

'Don't you smoke, Roland?'

'No. I'm not one for smoking. I don't smoke cigarettes and I don't smoke pot either.'

Inez came to the table and sat down the other side of him. Both the young men pressed food upon her. They started a laughing conversation together.

Mr Satterthwaite felt very happy among these young people. Not that they took very much notice of him apart from their natural politeness. But he liked hearing them. He liked, too, making up his judgement about them. He thought, he was almost sure, that both the young men were in love with Inez. Well, it was not surprising. Propinquity brings these things about. They had come to live here with their grandfather. A beautiful girl, Roland's first cousin, was living almost next door. Mr Satterthwaite turned his head. He could just see the house through the trees where it poked up from the road just beyond the front gate. That was the same house that Dr Horton had lived in last time he came here, seven or eight years ago.

He looked at Inez. He wondered which of the two young men she preferred or whether her affections were already engaged elsewhere. There was no reason why she should fall in love with one of these two attractive young specimens of the male race.

Having eaten as much as he wanted, it was not very much, Mr Satterthwaite drew his chair back altering its angle a little so that he could look all round him.

Mrs Gilliatt was still busy. Very much the housewife, he thought, making perhaps rather more of a fuss than she need of domesticity. Continually offering people cakes, taking their cups away and replenishing them, handing things round. Somehow, he thought, it would be more pleasant and more informal if she let people help themselves. He wished she was not so busy a hostess.

He looked up to the place where Tom Addison lay stretched out in his chair. Tom Addison was also watching Beryl Gilliatt. Mr Satterthwaite thought to himself: 'He doesn't like her. No. Tom doesn't like her. Well, perhaps that's to be expected.' After all, Beryl had taken the place of his own daughter, of Simon Gilliatt's first wife, Lily. 'My beautiful Lily,' thought Mr Satterthwaite again, and wondered why for some reason he felt that although he could not see anyone like her, yet Lily in some strange way was here. She was here at this tea party.

'I suppose one begins to imagine these things as one gets old,' said Mr Satterthwaite. 'After all, why shouldn't Lily be here to see her son.'

He looked affectionately at Timothy and then suddenly realized that he was not looking at Lily's son. Roland was Lily's son. Timothy was Beryl's son.

'I believe Lily knows I'm here. I believe she'd like to speak to me,' said Mr Satterthwaite. 'Oh dear, oh dear, I mustn't start imagining foolish things.'

For some reason he looked again at the scarecrow. It didn't look like a scarecrow now. It looked like Mr Harley Quin. Some tricks of the light, of the sunset, were providing it with colour, and there was a black dog like Hermes chasing the birds.

'Colour,' said Mr Satterthwaite, and looked again at the table and the tea set and the people having tea.

'Why am I here?' said Mr Satterthwaite to himself. 'Why am I here and what ought I to be doing? There's a reason . . .'

Now he knew, he felt, there was something, some crisis, something affecting – affecting all these people or only some of them? Beryl Gilliatt, Mrs Gilliatt. She was nervous about something. On edge. Tom? Nothing wrong with Tom. He wasn't affected. A lucky man to own this beauty, to own Doverton and to have a grandson so that when he died all this would come to Roland. All this would be Roland's. Was Tom hoping that Roland would marry Inez? Or would he have a fear of first cousins marrying? Though throughout history, Mr Satterthwaite thought, brothers had married sisters with no ill result. 'Nothing must happen,' said Mr Satterthwaite, 'nothing must happen. I must prevent it.'

Really, his thoughts were the thoughts of a madman. A peaceful scene. A tea set. The varying colours of the Harlequin cups. He looked at the white meerschaum pipe lying against the red of the cup. Beryl Gilliatt said something to Timothy. Timothy nodded, got up and went off towards the house. Beryl removed some empty plates from the table, adjusted a chair or two, murmured something to Roland, who went across and offered a frosted cake to Dr Horton.

Mr Satterthwaite watched her. He had to watch her.

The sweep of her sleeve as she passed the table. He saw a red cup get pushed off the table. It broke on the iron feet of a chair. He heard her little exclamation as she picked up the bits. She went to the tea tray, came back and placed on the table a pale blue cup and saucer. She replaced the meerschaum pipe, putting it close against it. She brought the teapot and poured tea, then she moved away.

The table was untenanted now. Inez also had got up and left it. Gone to speak to her grandfather. 'I don't understand,' said Mr Satterthwaite to himself. 'Something's going to happen. What's going to happen?'

A table with different coloured cups round, and – yes, Timothy, his red hair glowing in the sun. Red hair glowing with that same tint, that attractive sideways wave that Simon Gilliatt's hair had always had. Timothy, coming back, standing a moment, looking at the table with a slightly puzzled eye, then going to where the meerschaum pipe rested against the pale blue cup.

Inez came back then. She laughed suddenly and she said, 'Timothy, you're drinking your tea out of the wrong cup. The blue cup's mine. Yours is the red one.'

And Timothy said, 'Don't be silly, Inez, I know my own cup. It's got sugar in it and you won't like it. Nonsense. This is my cup. The meerschaum's up against it.'

It came to Mr Satterthwaite then. A shock. Was he mad? Was he imagining things? Was any of this real?

He got up. He walked quickly towards the table, and as Timothy raised the blue cup to his lips, he shouted.

'Don't drink that!' he called. 'Don't drink it, I say.'

Timothy turned a surprised face. Mr Satterthwaite turned his head. Dr Horton, rather startled, got up from his seat and was coming near.

'What's the matter, Satterthwaite?'

'That cup. There's something wrong about it,' said Mr Satterthwaite. 'Don't let the boy drink from it.'

Horton stared at it. 'My dear fellow –'

'I know what I'm saying. The red cup was his,' said Mr Satterthwaite, 'and the red cup's broken. It's been replaced with a blue one. He doesn't know the red from blue, does he?'

Dr Horton looked puzzled. 'D'you mean – d'you mean – like Tom?'

'Tom Addison. He's colour blind. You know that, don't you?'

'Oh yes, of course. We all know that. That's why he's got odd shoes on today. He never knew red from green.'

'This boy is the same.'

'But – but surely not. Anyway, there's never been any sign of it in – in Roland.'

'There might be, though, mightn't there?' said Mr Satterthwaite. 'I'm right in thinking – Daltonism. That's what they call it, don't they?'

'It was a name they used to call it by, yes.'

'It's not inherited by a female, but it passes through the female. Lily wasn't colour blind, but Lily's son might easily be colour blind.'

'But my dear Satterthwaite, Timothy isn't Lily's son. Roly is Lily's son. I know they're rather alike. Same age, same coloured hair and things, but – well, perhaps you don't remember.'

'No,' said Mr Satterthwaite, 'I shouldn't have remembered. But I know now. I can see the resemblance too. Roland's Beryl's son. They were both babies, weren't they, when Simon re-married. It is very easy for a woman looking after two babies, especially if both of them were going to have red hair. Timothy's Lily's son and Roland is Beryl's son. Beryl's and Christopher Eden's. There is no reason why he should be colour blind. I know it, I tell you. I know it!'

He saw Dr Horton's eyes go from one to the other. Timothy, not catching what they said but standing holding the blue cup and looking puzzled.

'I saw her buy it,' said Mr Satterthwaite. 'Listen to me, man. You must listen to me. You've known me for some years. You know that I don't make mistakes if I say a thing positively.'

'Quite true. I've never known you make a mistake.'

'Take that cup away from him,' said Mr Satterthwaite. 'Take it back to your surgery or take it to an analytic chemist and find out what's in it. I saw that woman buy that cup. She bought it in the village shop. She knew then that she was going to break a red cup, replace it by a blue and that Timothy would never know that the colours were different.'

'I think you're mad, Satterthwaite. But all the same I'm going to do what you say.'

He advanced on the table, stretched out a hand to the blue cup.

'Do you mind letting me have a look at that?' said Dr Horton.

'Of course,' said Timothy. He looked slightly surprised.

'I think there's a flaw in the china, here, you know. Rather interesting.'

Beryl came across the lawn. She came quickly and sharply.

'What are you doing? What's the matter? What is happening?'

'Nothing's the matter,' said Dr Horton, cheerfully. 'I just want to show the boys a little experiment I'm going to make with a cup of tea.'

He was looking at her very closely and he saw the

expression of fear, of terror. Mr Satterthwaite saw the entire change of countenance.

'Would you like to come with me, Satterthwaite? Just a little experiment, you know. A matter of testing porcelain and different qualities in it nowadays. A very interesting discovery was made lately.'

Chatting, he walked along the grass. Mr Satterthwaite followed him and the two young men, chatting to each other, followed him.

'What's the Doc up to now, Roly?' said Timothy.

'I don't know,' said Roland. 'He seems to have got some very extraordinary ideas. Oh well, we shall hear about it later, I expect. Let's go and get our bikes.'

Beryl Gilliatt turned abruptly. She retraced her steps rapidly up the lawn towards the house. Tom Addison called to her:

'Anything the matter, Beryl?'

'Something I'd forgotten,' said Beryl Gilliatt. 'That's all.'

Tom Addison looked inquiringly towards Simon Gilliatt.

'Anything wrong with your wife?' he said.

'Beryl? Oh no, not that I know of. I expect it's some little thing or other that she's forgotten. Nothing I can do for you, Beryl?' he called.

'No. No, I'll be back later.' She turned her head half sideways, looking at the old man lying back in the chair. She spoke suddenly and vehemently. 'You silly old fool. You've got the wrong shoes on again today. They don't match. Do you know you've got one shoe that's red and one shoe that's green?'

'Ah, done it again, have I?' said Tom Addison. 'They look exactly the same colour to me, you know. It's odd, isn't it, but there it is.'

She went past him, her steps quickening.

Presently Mr Satterthwaite and Dr Horton reached the gate that led out into the roadway. They heard a motor bicycle speeding along.

'She's gone,' said Dr Horton. 'She's run for it. We ought to have stopped her, I suppose. Do you think she'll come back?'

'No,' said Mr Satterthwaite, 'I don't think she'll come back. Perhaps,' he said thoughtfully, 'it's best left that way.'

'You mean?'

'It's an old house,' said Mr Satterthwaite. 'And old family. A good family. A lot of good people in it. One doesn't want trouble, scandal, everything brought upon it. Best to let her go, I think.'

'Tom Addison never liked her,' said Dr Horton. 'Never. He was always polite and kind but he didn't like her.'

'And there's the boy to think of,' said Mr Satterthwaite.

'The boy. You mean?'

'The other boy. Roland. This way he needn't know about what his mother was trying to do.'

'Why did she do it? Why on earth did she do it?'

'You've no doubt now that she did,' said Mr Satterthwaite.

'No. I've no doubt now. I saw her face, Satterthwaite, when she looked at me. I knew then that what you'd said was truth. But why?'

'Greed, I suppose,' said Mr Satterthwaite. 'She hadn't any money of her own, I believe. Her husband, Christopher Eden, was a nice chap by all accounts but he hadn't anything in the way of means. But Tom Addison's grandchild has got big money coming to him. A lot of money. Property all around here has appreciated enormously. I've no doubt that Tom Addison will leave the bulk of what he has to his grandson. She wanted it for her own son and through her own son, of course, for herself. She is a greedy woman.'

Mr Satterthwaite turned his head back suddenly.

'Something's on fire over there,' he said.

'Good lord, so it is. Oh, it's the scarecrow down in the field. Some young chap or other's set fire to it, I suppose. But there's nothing to worry about. There are no ricks or anything anywhere near. It'll just burn itself out.'

'Yes,' said Mr Satterthwaite. 'Well, you go on, Doctor. You don't need me to help you in your tests.'

'I've no doubt of what I shall find. I don't mean the exact substance, but I have come to your belief that this blue cup holds death.'

Mr Satterthwaite had turned back through the gate. He was going now down in the direction where the scarecrow was burning. Behind it was the sunset. A remarkable sunset that evening. Its colours illuminated the air round it, illuminated the burning scarecrow.

'So that's the way you've chosen to go,' said Mr Satterthwaite.

He looked slightly startled then, for in the neighbourhood of the flames he saw the tall, slight figure of a woman. A woman dressed in some pale mother-of-pearl colouring. She was walking in the direction of Mr Satterthwaite. He stopped dead, watching.

'Lily,' he said. 'Lily.'

He saw her quite plainly now. It was Lily walking towards him. Too far away for him to see her face but he knew very well who it was. Just for a moment or two he wondered whether anyone else would see her or whether the sight was only for him. He said, not very loud, only in a whisper,

'It's all right, Lily, your son is safe.'

She stopped then. She raised one hand to her lips. He didn't see her smile, but he knew she was smiling. She kissed her hand and waved it to him and then she turned. She walked back towards where the scarecrow was disintegrating into a mass of ashes.

'She's going away again,' said Mr Satterthwaite to himself. 'She's going away with him. They're walking away together. They belong to the same world, of course. They only come – those sort of people – they only come when it's a case of love or death or both.'

He wouldn't see Lily again, he supposed, but he wondered how soon he would meet Mr Quin again. He turned then and went back across the lawn towards the tea table and the Harlequin tea set, and beyond that, to his old friend Tom Addison. Beryl wouldn't come back. He was sure of it. Doverton Kingsbourne was safe again.

Across the lawn came the small black dog in flying leaps. It came to Mr Satterthwaite, panting a little and wagging its tail. Through its collar was twisted a scrap of paper. Mr Satterthwaite stooped and detached it – smoothing it out – on it in coloured letters was written a message:

CONGRATULATIONS! TO OUR NEXT MEETING

H.Q.

'Thank you, Hermes,' said Mr Satterthwaite, and watched the black dog flying across the meadow to rejoin the two figures that he himself knew were there but could no longer see.

The Regatta Mystery

I

Mr Isaac Pointz removed a cigar from his lips and said approvingly:

'Pretty little place.'

Having thus set the seal of his approval upon Dartmouth harbour, he replaced the cigar and looked about him with the air of a man pleased with himself, his appearance, his surroundings and life generally.

As regards the first of these, Mr Isaac Pointz was a man of fifty-eight, in good health and condition with perhaps a slight tendency to liver. He was not exactly stout, but comfortable-looking, and a yachting costume, which he wore at the moment, is not the most kindly of attires for a middle-aged man with a tendency to embonpoint. Mr Pointz was very well turned out – correct to every crease and button – his dark and slightly Oriental face beaming out under the peak of his yachting cap. As regards his surroundings, these may have been taken to mean his companions – his partner Mr Leo Stein, Sir George and Lady Marroway, an American business acquaintance Mr Samuel Leathern and his schoolgirl daughter Eve, Mrs Rustington and Evan Llewellyn.

The party had just come ashore from Mr Pointz' yacht – the *Merrimaid.* In the morning they had watched the yacht racing and they had now come ashore to join for a while in the fun of the fair – Coconut shies, Fat Ladies, the Human Spider and the Merry-go-round. It is hardly to be doubted that these delights were relished most by Eve Leathern. When Mr Pointz finally suggested that it was time to adjourn to the Royal George for dinner hers was the only dissentient voice.

'Oh, Mr Pointz – I did so want to have my fortune told by the Real Gypsy in the Caravan.'

Mr Pointz had doubts of the essential Realness of the Gypsy in question but he gave indulgent assent.

'Eve's just crazy about the fair,' said her father apologetically. 'But don't you pay any attention if you want to be getting along.'

'Plenty of time,' said Mr Pointz benignantly. 'Let the little lady enjoy herself. I'll take you on at darts, Leo.'

'Twenty-five and over wins a prize,' chanted the man in charge of the darts in a high nasal voice.

'Bet you a fiver my total score beats yours,' said Pointz.

'Done,' said Stein with alacrity.

The two men were soon whole-heartedly engaged in their battle.

Lady Marroway murmured to Evan Llewellyn:

'Eve is not the only child in the party.'

Llewellyn smiled assent but somewhat absently.

He had been absent-minded all that day. Once or twice his answers had been wide of the point.

Pamela Marroway drew away from him and said to her husband:

'That young man has something on his mind.'

Sir George murmured:

'Or someone?'

And his glance swept quickly over Janet Rustington.

Lady Marroway frowned a little. She was a tall woman exquisitely groomed. The scarlet of her fingernails was matched by the dark red coral studs in her ears. Her eyes were dark and watchful. Sir George affected a careless 'hearty English gentleman' manner – but his bright blue eyes held the same watchful look as his wife's.

Isaac Pointz and Leo Stein were Hatton Garden diamond merchants. Sir George and Lady Marroway came from a different world – the world of Antibes and Juan les Pins – of golf at St Jean-de-Luz – of bathing from the rocks at Madeira in the winter.

In outward seeming they were as the lilies that toiled not, neither did they spin. But perhaps this was not quite true. There are diverse ways of toiling and also of spinning.

'Here's the kid back again,' said Evan Llewellyn to Mrs Rustington.

He was a dark young man – there was a faintly hungry wolfish look about him which some women found attractive.

It was difficult to say whether Mrs Rustington found him so. She did not wear her heart on her sleeve. She had married young – and the marriage had ended in disaster in less than a year. Since that time it was difficult to know what Janet Rustington thought of anyone or anything – her manner was always the same – charming but completely aloof.

Eve Leathern came dancing up to them, her lank fair hair bobbing excitedly. She was fifteen – an awkward child – but full of vitality.

'I'm going to be married by the time I'm seventeen,' she exclaimed breathlessly. 'To a very rich man and we're going to have six children and Tuesdays and Thursdays are my lucky days and I ought always to wear green or blue and an emerald is my lucky stone and –'

'Why, pet, I think we ought to be getting along,' said her father.

Mr Leathern was a tall, fair, dyspeptic-looking man with a somewhat mournful expression.

Mr Pointz and Mr Stein were turning away from the darts. Mr Pointz was chuckling and Mr Stein was looking somewhat rueful.

'It's all a matter of luck,' he was saying.

Mr Pointz slapped his pocket cheerfully.

'Took a fiver off you all right. Skill, my boy, skill. My old Dad was a first class darts player. Well, folks, let's be getting along. Had your fortune told, Eve? Did they tell you to beware of a dark man?'

'A dark woman,' corrected Eve. 'She's got a cast in her eye and she'll be real mean to me if I give her a chance. And I'm to be married by the time I'm seventeen . . .'

She ran on happily as the party steered its way to the Royal George.

Dinner had been ordered beforehand by the forethought of Mr Pointz and a bowing waiter led them upstairs and into a private room on the first floor. Here a round table was ready laid. The big bulging bow-window opened on the harbour square and was open. The noise of the fair came up to them, and the raucous squeal of three roundabouts each blaring a different tune.

'Best shut that if we're to hear ourselves speak,' observed Mr Pointz drily, and suited the action to the word.

They took their seats round the table and Mr Pointz beamed affectionately at his guests. He felt he was doing them well and he liked to do people well. His eye rested on one after another. Lady Marroway – fine woman – not quite the goods, of course, he knew that – he was perfectly well aware that what he had called all his life the *crême de la crême* would have very little to do with the Marroways – but then the *crême de la crême* were supremely unaware of his own existence. Anyway, Lady Marroway was a damned smart-looking woman – and he didn't mind if she *did* rook him at Bridge. Didn't enjoy it quite so much from Sir George. Fishy eye the fellow had. Brazenly on the make. But he wouldn't make too much out of Isaac Pointz. He'd see to that all right.

Old Leathern wasn't a bad fellow – longwinded, of course, like most Americans – fond of telling endless long stories. And he had that disconcerting habit of requiring precise information. What was the population of Dartmouth? In what year had the Naval College been built? And so on. Expected his host to be a kind of walking Baedeker. Eve was a nice cheery kid – he enjoyed chaffing her. Voice rather like a corncake, but she had all her wits about her. A bright kid.

Young Llewellyn – he seemed a bit quiet. Looked as though he had something on his mind. Hard up, probably. These writing fellows usually were. Looked as though he might be keen on Janet Rustington. A nice woman – attractive and clever, too. But she didn't ram her writing down your throat. Highbrow sort of stuff she wrote but you'd never think it to hear her talk. And old Leo! *He* wasn't getting younger or thinner. And blissfully unaware that his partner was at that moment thinking precisely the same thing about him, Mr Pointz corrected Mr Leathern as to pilchards being connected with Devon and not Cornwall, and prepared to enjoy his dinner.

'Mr Pointz,' said Eve when plates of hot mackerel had been set before them and the waiters had left the room.

'Yes, young lady.'

'Have you got that big diamond with you right now? The one you showed us last night and said you always took about with you?'

Mr Pointz chuckled.

'That's right. My mascot, I call it. Yes, I've got it with me all right.'

'I think that's awfully dangerous. Somebody might get it away from you in the crowd at the fair.'

'Not they,' said Mr Pointz. 'I'll take good care of that.'

'But they *might*,' insisted Eve. 'You've got gangsters in England as well as we have, haven't you?'

'They won't get the Morning Star,' said Mr Pointz.

'To begin with it's in a special inner pocket. And anyway – old Pointz knows what he's about. Nobody's going to steal the Morning Star.'

Eve laughed.

'Ugh-huh – bet I could steal it!'

'I bet you couldn't.' Mr Pointz twinkled back at her.

'Well, I bet I could. I was thinking about it last night in bed – after you'd handed it round the table, for us all to look at. I thought of a real cute way to steal it.'

'And what's that?'

Eve put her head on one side, her fair hair wagged excitedly. 'I'm not telling you – now. What do you bet I couldn't?'

Memories of Mr Pointz's youth rose in his mind.

'Half a dozen pairs of gloves,' he said.

'Gloves,' cried Eve disgustedly. 'Who wears gloves?'

'Well – do you wear nylon stockings?'

'Do I not? My best pair ran this morning.'

'Very well, then. Half a dozen pairs of the finest nylon stockings –'

'Oo-er,' said Eve blissfully. 'And what about you?'

'Well, I need a new tobacco pouch.'

'Right. That's a deal. Not that you'll get your tobacco pouch. Now I'll tell you what you've got to do. You must hand it round like you did last night –'

She broke off as two waiters entered to remove the

plates. When they were starting on the next course of chicken, Mr Pointz said:

'Remember this, young woman, if this is to represent a real theft, I should send for the police and you'd be searched.'

'That's quite OK by me. You needn't be quite so lifelike as to bring the police into it. But Lady Marroway or Mrs Rustington can do all the searching you like.'

'Well, that's that then,' said Mr Pointz. 'What are you setting up to be? A first class jewel thief?'

'I might take to it as a career – if it really paid.'

'If you got away with the Morning Star it would pay you. Even after recutting that stone would be worth over thirty thousand pounds.'

'My!' said Eve, impressed. 'What's that in dollars?'

Lady Marroway uttered an exclamation.

'And you carry such a stone about with you?' she said reproachfully. 'Thirty thousand pounds.' Her darkened eyelashes quivered.

Mrs Rustington said softly: 'It's a lot of money . . . And then there's the fascination of the stone itself . . . It's beautiful.'

'Just a piece of carbon,' said Evan Llewellyn.

'I've always understood it's the "fence" that's the difficulty in jewel robberies,' said Sir George. 'He takes the lion's share – eh, what?'

'Come on,' said Eve excitedly. 'Let's start. Take the diamond out and say what you said last night.'

Mr Leathern said in his deep melancholy voice, 'I do apologize for my offspring. She gets kinder worked up –'

'That'll do, Pops,' said Eve. 'Now then, Mr Pointz –'

Smiling, Mr Pointz fumbled in an inner pocket. He drew something out. It lay on the palm of his hand, blinking in the light.

'A diamond . . .'

Rather stiffly, Mr Pointz repeated as far as he could remember his speech of the previous evening on the *Merrimaid*.

'Perhaps you ladies and gentlemen would like to have a look at this? It's an unusually beautiful stone. I call it the Morning Star and it's by way of being my mascot – goes about with me anywhere. Like to see it?'

He handed it to Lady Marroway, who took it, exclaimed at its beauty and passed it to Mr Leathern who said, 'Pretty good – yes, pretty good,' in a somewhat artificial manner and in his turn passed it to Llewellyn.

The waiters coming in at that moment, there was a slight hitch in the proceedings. When they had gone again, Evan said, 'Very fine stone,' and passed it to Leo Stein who did not trouble to make any comment but handed it quickly on to Eve.

'How perfectly lovely,' cried Eve in a high affected voice.

'Oh!' She gave a cry of consternation as it slipped from her hand. 'I've dropped it.'

She pushed back her chair and got down to grope under the table. Sir George at her right, bent also. A glass got swept off the table in the confusion. Stein, Llewellyn and Mrs Rustington all helped in the search. Finally Lady Marroway joined in.

Only Mr Pointz took no part in the proceedings. He remained in his seat sipping his wine and smiling sardonically.

'Oh, dear,' said Eve, still in her artificial manner, 'How dreadful! Where *can* it have rolled to? I can't find it anywhere.'

One by one the assistant searchers rose to their feet.

'It's disappeared all right, Pointz,' said Sir George smiling.

'Very nicely done,' said Mr Pointz, nodding approval. 'You'd make a very good actress, Eve. Now the question is, have you hidden it somewhere or have you got it on you?'

'Search me,' said Eve dramatically.

Mr Pointz' eye sought out a large screen in the corner of the room.

He nodded towards it and then looked at Lady Marroway and Mrs Rustington.

'If you ladies will be so good –'

'Why, certainly,' said Lady Marroway, smiling.

The two women rose.

Lady Marroway said, 'Don't be afraid, Mr Pointz. We'll vet her properly.'

The three went behind the screen.

The room was hot. Evan Llewellyn flung open the window. A news vendor was passing. Evan threw down a coin and the man threw up a paper.

Llewellyn unfolded it.

'Hungarian situation's none too good,' he said.

'That the local rag?' asked Sir George. 'There's a horse I'm interested in ought to have run at Haldon today – Natty Boy.'

'Leo,' said Mr Pointz. 'Lock the door. We don't want those damned waiters popping in and out till this business is over.'

'Natty Boy won three to one,' said Evan.

'Rotten odds,' said Sir George.

'Mostly Regatta news,' said Evan, glancing over the sheet.

The three young women came out from the screen.

'Not a sign of it,' said Janet Rustington.

'You can take it from me she hasn't got it on her,' said Lady Marroway.

Mr Pointz thought he would be quite ready to take it from her. There was a grim tone in her voice and he felt no doubt that the search had been thorough.

'Say, Eve, you haven't swallowed it?' asked Mr Leathern anxiously. 'Because maybe that wouldn't be too good for you.'

'I'd have seen her do that,' said Leo Stein quietly. 'I was watching her. She didn't put anything in her mouth.'

'I couldn't swallow a great thing all points like that,' said Eve. She put her hands on her hips and looked at Mr Pointz. 'What about it, big boy?' she asked.

'You stand over there where you are and don't move,' said that gentleman.

Among them, the men stripped the table and turned it upside down. Mr Pointz examined every inch of it. Then he transferred his attention to the chair on which Eve had been sitting and those on either side of her.

The thoroughness of the search left nothing to be desired. The other four men joined in and the women also. Eve Leathern stood by the wall near the screen and laughed with intense enjoyment.

Five minutes later Mr Pointz rose with a slight groan from his knees and dusted his trousers sadly. His pristine freshness was somewhat impaired.

'Eve,' he said. 'I take off my hat to you. You're the finest thing in jewel thieves I've ever come across. What you've done with that stone beats me. As far as I can see it must be in the room as it isn't on you. I give you best.'

'Are the stockings mine?' demanded Eve.

'They're yours, young lady.'

'Eve, my child, where *can* you have hidden it?' demanded Mrs Rustington curiously.

Eve pranced forward.

'I'll show you. You'll all be just mad with yourselves.'

She went across to the side table where the things from the dinner table had been roughly stacked. She picked up her little black evening bag –

'Right under your eyes. Right . . .'

Her voice, gay and triumphant, trailed off suddenly.

'Oh,' she said. '*Oh . . .*'

'What's the matter, honey?' said her father.

Eve whispered: 'It's gone . . . it's *gone . . .*'

'What's all this?' asked Pointz, coming forward.

Eve turned to him impetuously.

'It was like this. This pochette of mine has a big paste stone in the middle of the clasp. It fell out last night and just when you were showing that diamond round I noticed that it was much the same size. And so I thought in the night what a good idea for a robbery it would be to wedge your diamond into the gap with a bit of plasticine. I felt sure nobody would ever spot it. That's what I did tonight. First I dropped it – then went down after it with the bag in my hand, stuck it into the gap with a bit of plasticine which I had handy, put my bag on the table and went on pretending to look for the diamond. I thought it would be like the Purloined Letter – you know – lying there in full view under all your noses – and just looking like a common bit of rhinestone. And it was a good plan – none of you *did* notice.'

'I wonder,' said Mr Stein.

'What did you say?'

Mr Pointz took the bag, looked at the empty hole with a fragment of plasticine still adhering to it and said slowly: 'It may have fallen out. We'd better look again.'

The search was repeated, but this time it was a curiously silent business. An atmosphere of tension pervaded the room.

Finally everyone in turn gave it up. They stood looking at each other.

'It's not in this room,' said Stein.

'And nobody's left the room,' said Sir George significantly.

There was a moment's pause. Eve burst into tears.

Her father patted her on the shoulder.

'There, there,' he said awkwardly.

Sir George turned to Leo Stein.

'Mr Stein,' he said. 'Just now you murmured something under your breath. When I asked you to repeat it, you said it was nothing. But as a matter of fact I heard what you said. Miss Eve had just said that none of us noticed the place where she had put the diamond. The words you murmured were: "I wonder." What we have to face is the probability that one person *did* notice – that that person is in this room now. I suggest that the only fair and honourable thing is for every one present to submit to a search. The diamond cannot have left the room.'

When Sir George played the part of the old English gentleman, none could play it better. His voice rang with sincerity and indignation.

'Bit unpleasant, all this,' said Mr Pointz unhappily.

'It's all my fault,' sobbed Eve. 'I didn't mean –'

'Buck up, kiddo,' said Mr Stein kindly. 'Nobody's blaming you.'

Mr Leathern said in his slow pedantic manner:

'Why, certainly, I think that Sir George's suggestion will meet with the fullest approval from all of us. It does from me.'

'I agree,' said Evan Llewellyn.

Mrs Rustington looked at Lady Marroway who nodded a brief assent. The two of them went back behind the screen and the sobbing Eve accompanied them.

A waiter knocked on the door and was told to go away.

Five minutes later eight people looked at each other incredulously.

The Morning Star had vanished into space . . .

II

Mr Parker Pyne looked thoughtfully at the dark agitated face of the young man opposite him.

'Of course,' he said. 'You're Welsh, Mr Llewellyn.'

'What's that got to do with it?'

Mr Parker Pyne waved a large, well-cared-for hand.

'Nothing at all, I admit. I am interested in the classification of emotional reactions as exemplified by certain racial types. That is all. Let us return to the consideration of your particular problem.'

'I don't really know why I came to you,' said Evan Llewellyn. His hands twitched nervously, and his dark face had a haggard look. He did not look at Mr Parker Pyne and that gentleman's scrutiny seemed to make him uncomfortable. 'I don't know why I came to you,' he repeated. 'But where the Hell *can* I go? And what the Hell can I *do*? It's the powerlessness of not being able to do anything at all that gets me . . . I saw your advertisement and I remembered that a chap had once spoken of you and said that you got results . . . And – well – I came! I suppose

I was a fool. It's the sort of position nobody can do anything about.'

'Not at all,' said Mr Parker Pyne. 'I am the proper person to come to. I am a specialist in unhappiness. This business has obviously caused you a good deal of pain. You are sure the facts are exactly as you have told me?'

'I don't think I've left out anything. Pointz brought out the diamond and passed it around – that wretched American child stuck it on her ridiculous bag and when we came to look at the bag, the diamond was gone. It wasn't on anyone – old Pointz himself even was searched – he suggested it himself – and I'll swear it was nowhere in that room! *And nobody left the room* –'

'No waiters, for instance?' suggested Mr Parker Pyne.

Llewellyn shook his head.

'They went out before the girl began messing about with the diamond, and afterwards Pointz locked the door so as to keep them out. No, it lies between one of us.'

'It would certainly seem so,' said Mr Parker Pyne thoughtfully.

'That damned evening paper,' said Evan Llewellyn bitterly. 'I saw it come into their minds – that that was the only way –'

'Just tell me again exactly what occurred.'

'It was perfectly simple. I threw open the window, whistled to the man, threw down a copper and he tossed me up the paper. And there it is, you see – the only possible way the diamond could have left the room – thrown by me to an accomplice waiting in the street below.'

'Not the *only* possible way,' said Mr Parker Pyne.

'What other way can you suggest?'

'If you didn't throw it out, there *must* have been some other way.'

'Oh, I see. I hoped you meant something more definite than that. Well, I can only say that I *didn't* throw it out. I can't expect you to believe me – or anyone else.'

'Oh, yes, I believe you,' said Mr Parker Pyne.

'You do? Why?'

'Not a criminal type,' said Mr Parker Pyne. 'Not, that is, the particular criminal type that steals jewellery. There are crimes, of course, that you might commit – but we won't enter into that subject. At any rate I do not see you as the purloiner of the Morning Star.'

'Everyone else does though,' said Llewellyn bitterly.

'I see,' said Mr Parker Pyne.

'They looked at me in a queer sort of way at the time. Marroway picked up the paper and just glanced over at the window. He didn't say anything. But Pointz cottoned on to it quick enough! I could see what they thought. There hasn't been any open accusation, that's the devil of it.'

Mr Parker Pyne nodded sympathetically.

'It is worse than that,' he said.

'Yes. It's just suspicion. I've had a fellow round asking questions – routine inquiries, he called it. One of the new dress-shirted lot of police, I suppose. Very tactful – nothing at all hinted. Just interested in the fact that I'd been hard up and was suddenly cutting a bit of a splash.'

'And were you?'

'Yes – some luck with a horse or two. Unluckily my bets were made on the course – there's nothing to show that that's how the money came in. They can't disprove it, of course – but that's just the sort of easy lie a fellow would invent if he didn't want to show where the money came from.'

'I agree. Still they will have to have a good deal more than that to go upon.'

'Oh! I'm not afraid of actually being arrested and charged with the theft. In a way that would be easier – one would know, where one was. It's the ghastly fact that all those people believe I took it.'

'One person in particular?'

'What do you mean?'

'A suggestion – nothing more –' Again Mr Parker Pyne waved his comfortable-looking hand. 'There *was* one person in particular, wasn't there? Shall we say Mrs Rustington?'

Llewellyn's dark face flushed.

'Why pitch on her?'

'Oh, my dear sir – there is obviously someone whose opinion matters to you greatly – probably a lady. What ladies were there? An American flapper? Lady Marroway? But you would probably rise not fall in Lady Marroway's estimation if you had brought off such a coup. I know something of the lady. Clearly then, Mrs Rustington.'

Llewellyn said with something of an effort,

'She – she's had rather an unfortunate experience. Her husband was a down and out rotter. It's made her unwilling to trust anyone. She – if she thinks –'

He found it difficult to go on.

'Quite so,' said Mr Parker Pyne. 'I see the matter is important. It must be cleared up.'

Evan gave a short laugh.

'That's easy to say.'

'And quite easy to do,' said Mr Parker Pyne.

'You think so?'

'Oh, yes – the problem is so clear cut. So many possibilities are ruled out. The answer must really be extremely simple. Indeed already I have a kind of glimmering –'

Llewellyn stared at him incredulously.

Mr Parker Pyne drew a pad of paper towards him and picked up a pen.

'Perhaps you would give me a brief description of the party.'

'Haven't I already done so?'

'Their personal appearance – colour of hair and so on.'

'But, Mr Parker Pyne, what can that have to do with it?'

'A good deal, young man, a good deal. Classification and so on.'

Somewhat unbelievingly, Evan described the personal appearance of the members of the yachting party.

Mr Parker Pyne made a note or two, pushed away the pad and said:

'Excellent. By the way, did you say a wine glass was broken?'

Evan stared again.

'Yes, it was knocked off the table and then it got stepped on.'

'Nasty thing, splinters of glass,' said Mr Parker Pyne. 'Whose wine glass was it?'

'I think it was the child's – Eve.'

'Ah! – and who sat next to her on that side?'

'Sir George Marroway.'

'You didn't see which of them knocked it off the table?'

'Afraid I didn't. Does it matter?'

'Not really. No. That was a superfluous question. Well' – he stood up – 'good morning, Mr Llewellyn. Will you call again in three days' time? I think the whole thing will be quite satisfactorily cleared up by then.'

'Are you joking, Mr Parker Pyne?'

'I never joke on professional matters, my dear sir. It would occasion distrust in my clients. Shall we say Friday at eleven-thirty? Thank you.'

III

Evan entered Mr Parker Pyne's office on the Friday morning in a considerable turmoil. Hope and scepticism fought for mastery.

Mr Parker Pyne rose to meet him with a beaming smile.

'Good morning, Mr Llewellyn. Sit down. Have a cigarette?'

Llewellyn waved aside the proffered box.

'Well?' he said.

'Very well indeed,' said Mr Parker Pyne. 'The police arrested the gang last night.'

'The gang? What gang?'

'The Amalfi gang. I thought of them at once when you told me your story. I recognized their methods and once you had described the guests, well, there was no doubt at all in my mind.'

'Who are the Amalfi gang?'

'Father, son and daughter-in-law – that is if Pietro and Maria are really married – which some doubt.'

'I don't understand.'

'It's quite simple. The name is Italian and no doubt the origin is Italian, but old Amalfi was born in America. His methods are usually the same. He impersonates a real business man, introduces himself to some prominent figure in the jewel business in some European country and then plays his little trick. In this case he was deliberately on the track of the Morning Star. Pointz' idiosyncrasy was well known in the trade. Maria Amalfi played the part of his daughter (amazing creature, twenty-seven at least, and nearly always plays a part of sixteen).'

'Not Eve!' gasped Llewellyn.

'Exactly. The third member of the gang got himself taken on as an extra waiter at the Royal George – it was holiday time, remember, and they would need extra staff. He may even have bribed a regular man to stay away. The scene is set. Eve challenges old Pointz and he takes on the bet. He passes round the diamond as he had done the night before. The waiters enter the room and Leathern retains the stone until they have left the room. When they do leave, the diamond leaves also, neatly attached with a morsel of chewing gum to the underside of the plate that Pietro bears away. So simple!'

'But I *saw* it after that.'

'No, no, you saw a paste replica, good enough to deceive a casual glance. Stein, you told me, hardly looked at it. Eve drops it, sweeps off a glass too and steps firmly on stone and glass together. Miraculous disappearance of diamond. Both Eve and Leathern can submit to as much searching as anyone pleases.'

'Well – I'm –' Evan shook his head, at a loss for words.

'You say you recognized the gang from my description. Had they worked this trick before?'

'Not exactly – but it was their kind of business. Naturally my attention was at once directed to the girl Eve.'

'Why? I didn't suspect her – nobody did. She seemed such a – such a *child*.'

'That is the peculiar genius of Maria Amalfi. She is more like a child than any child could possibly be! And then the plasticine! This bet was supposed to have arisen quite spontaneously – yet the little lady had some plasticine with her all handy. That spoke of premeditation. My suspicions fastened on her at once.'

Llewellyn rose to his feet.

'Well, Mr Parker Pyne, I'm no end obliged to you.'

'Classification,' murmured Mr Parker Pyne. 'The classification of criminal types – it interests me.'

'You'll let me know how much – er –'

'My fee will be quite moderate,' said Mr Parker Pyne. 'It will not make too big a hole in the – er – horse racing profits. All the same, young man, I should, I think, leave the horses alone in future. Very uncertain animal, the horse.'

'That's all right,' said Evan.

He shook Mr Parker Pyne by the hand and strode from the office.

He hailed a taxi and gave the address of Janet Rustington's flat.

He felt in a mood to carry all before him.

The Love Detectives

I

Little Mr Satterthwaite looked thoughtfully across at his host. The friendship between these two men was an odd one. The colonel was a simple country gentleman whose passion in life was sport. The few weeks that he spent perforce in London, he spent unwillingly. Mr Satterthwaite, on the other hand, was a town bird. He was an authority on French cooking, on ladies' dress, and on all the latest scandals. His passion was observing human nature, and he was an expert in his own special line – that of an onlooker at life.

It would seem, therefore, that he and Colonel Melrose would have little in common, for the colonel had no interest in his neighbours' affairs and a horror of any kind of emotion. The two men were friends mainly because their fathers before them had been friends. Also they knew the same people and had reactionary views about *nouveaux riches*.

It was about half past seven. The two men were sitting in the colonel's comfortable study, and Melrose was describing a run of the previous winter with a keen hunting man's enthusiasm. Mr Satterthwaite, whose knowledge of horses consisted chiefly of the time-honoured Sunday morning visit to the stables which still obtains in old-fashioned country houses, listened with his invariable politeness.

The sharp ringing of the telephone interrupted Melrose. He crossed to the table and took up the receiver.

'Hello, yes – Colonel Melrose speaking. What's that?' His whole demeanour altered – became stiff and official. It was the magistrate speaking now, not the sportsman.

He listened for some moments, then said laconically, 'Right, Curtis. I'll be over at once.' He replaced the receiver and turned to his guest. 'Sir James Dwighton has been found in his library – murdered.'

'What?'

Mr Satterthwaite was startled – thrilled.

'I must go over to Alderway at once. Care to come with me?'

Mr Satterthwaite remembered that the colonel was chief constable of the county.

'If I shan't be in the way –' He hesitated.

'Not at all. That was Inspector Curtis telephoning.

Good, honest fellow, but no brains. I'd be glad if you would come with me, Satterthwaite. I've got an idea this is going to turn out a nasty business.'

'Have they got the fellow who did it?'

'No,' replied Melrose shortly.

Mr Satterthwaite's trained ear detected a nuance of reserve behind the curt negative. He began to go over in his mind all that he knew of the Dwightons.

A pompous old fellow, the late Sir James, brusque in his manner. A man that might easily make enemies. Veering on sixty, with grizzled hair and a florid face. Reputed to be tight-fisted in the extreme.

His mind went on to Lady Dwighton. Her image floated before him, young, auburn-haired, slender. He remembered various rumours, hints, odd bits of gossip. So that was it – that was why Melrose looked so glum. Then he pulled himself up – his imagination was running away with him.

Five minutes later Mr Satterthwaite took his place beside his host in the latter's little two seater, and they drove off together into the night.

The colonel was a taciturn man. They had gone quite a mile and a half before he spoke. Then he jerked out abruptly. 'You know 'em, I suppose?'

'The Dwightons? I know all about them, of course.' Who was there Mr Satterthwaite didn't know all about? 'I've met him once, I think, and her rather oftener.'

'Pretty woman,' said Melrose.

'Beautiful!' declared Mr Satterthwaite.

'Think so?'

'A pure Renaissance type,' declared Mr Satterthwaite, warming up to his theme. 'She acted in those theatricals – the charity matinee, you know, last spring. I was very much struck. Nothing modern about her – a pure survival. One can imagine her in the doge's palace, or as Lucrezia Borgia.'

The colonel let the car swerve slightly, and Mr Satterthwaite came to an abrupt stop. He wondered what fatality had brought the name of Lucrezia Borgia to his tongue. Under the circumstances –

'Dwighton was not poisoned, was he?' he asked abruptly.

Melrose looked at him sideways, somewhat curiously. 'Why do you ask that, I wonder?' he said.

'Oh, I – I don't know.' Mr Satterthwaite was flustered. 'I – It just occurred to me.'

'Well, he wasn't,' said Melrose gloomily. 'If you want to know, he was crashed on the head.'

'With a blunt instrument,' murmured Mr Satterthwaite, nodding his head sagely.

'Don't talk like a damned detective story, Satterthwaite. He was hit on the head with a bronze figure.'

'Oh,' said Satterthwaite, and relapsed into silence.

'Know anything of a chap called Paul Delangua?'

asked Melrose after a minute or two.

'Yes. Good-looking young fellow.'

'I daresay women would call him so,' growled the colonel.

'You don't like him?'

'No, I don't.'

'I should have thought you would have. He rides very well.'

'Like a foreigner at the horse show. Full of monkey tricks.'

Mr Satterthwaite suppressed a smile. Poor old Melrose was so very British in his outlook. Agreeably conscious himself of a cosmopolitan point of view, Mr Satterthwaite was able to deplore the insular attitude toward life.

'Has he been down in this part of the world?' he asked.

'He's been staying at Alderway with the Dwightons. The rumour goes that Sir James kicked him out a week ago.'

'Why?'

'Found him making love to his wife, I suppose. What the hell –'

There was a violent swerve, and a jarring impact.

'Most dangerous crossroads in England,' said Melrose. 'All the same, the other fellow should have sounded his horn. We're on the main road. I fancy we've damaged him rather more than he has damaged us.'

He sprang out. A figure alighted from the other car and joined him. Fragments of speech reached Satterthwaite.

'Entirely my fault, I'm afraid,' the stranger was saying. 'But I do not know this part of the country very well, and there's absolutely no sign of any kind to show you're coming onto the main road.'

The colonel, mollified, rejoined suitably. The two men bent together over the stranger's car, which a chauffeur was already examining. The conversation became highly technical.

'A matter of half an hour, I'm afraid,' said the stranger. 'But don't let me detain you. I'm glad your car escaped injury as well as it did.'

'As a matter of fact –' the colonel was beginning, but he was interrupted.

Mr Satterthwaite, seething with excitement, hopped out of the car with a birdlike action, and seized the stranger warmly by the hand.

'It *is!* I thought I recognized the voice,' he declared excitedly. 'What an extraordinary thing. What a very extraordinary thing.'

'Eh?' said Colonel Melrose.

'Mr Harley Quin. Melrose, I'm sure you've heard me speak many times of Mr Quin?'

Colonel Melrose did not seem to remember the

fact, but he assisted politely at the scene while Mr Satterthwaite was chirruping gaily on. 'I haven't seen you – let me see –'

'Since the night at the Bells and Motley,' said the other quietly.

'The Bells and Motley, eh?' said the colonel.

'An inn,' explained Mr Satterthwaite.

'What an odd name for an inn.'

'Only an old one,' said Mr Quin. 'There was a time, remember, when bells and motley were more common in England than they are nowadays.'

'I suppose so, yes, no doubt you are right,' said Melrose vaguely. He blinked. By a curious effect of light – the headlights of one car and the red tail-light of the other – Mr Quin seemed for a moment to be dressed in motley himself. But it was only the light.

'We can't leave you here stranded on the road,' continued Mr Satterthwaite. 'You must come along with us. There's plenty of room for three, isn't there, Melrose?'

'Oh rather.' But the colonel's voice was a little doubtful. 'The only thing is,' he remarked, 'the job we're on. Eh, Satterthwaite?'

Mr Satterthwaite stood stock-still. Ideas leaped and flashed over him. He positively shook with excitement.

'No,' he cried. 'No, I should have known better!

There is no chance where you are concerned, Mr Quin. It was not an accident that we all met tonight at the crossroads.'

Colonel Melrose stared at his friend in astonishment. Mr Satterthwaite took him by the arm.

'You remember what I told you – about our friend Derek Capel? The motive for his suicide, which no one could guess? It was Mr Quin who solved that problem – and there have been others since. He shows you things that are there all the time, but which you haven't seen. He's marvellous.'

'My dear Satterthwaite, you are making me blush,' said Mr Quin, smiling. 'As far as I can remember, these discoveries were all made by you, not by me.'

'They were made because you were there,' said Mr Satterthwaite with intense conviction.

'Well,' said Colonel Melrose, clearing his throat uncomfortably. 'We mustn't waste any more time. Let's get on.'

He climbed into the driver's seat. He was not too well pleased at having the stranger foisted upon him through Mr Satterthwaite's enthusiasm, but he had no valid objection to offer, and he was anxious to get on to Alderway as fast as possible.

Mr Satterthwaite urged Mr Quin in next, and himself took the outside seat. The car was a roomy one and took three without undue squeezing.

'So you are interested in crime, Mr Quin?' said the colonel, doing his best to be genial.

'No, not exactly in crime.'

'What, then?'

Mr Quin smiled. 'Let us ask Mr Satterthwaite. He is a very shrewd observer.'

'I think,' said Satterthwaite slowly, 'I may be wrong, but I think – that Mr Quin is interested in – lovers.'

He blushed as he said the last word, which is one no Englishman can pronounce without self-consciousness. Mr Satterthwaite brought it out apologetically, and with an effect of inverted commas.

'By gad!' said the colonel, startled and silenced.

He reflected inwardly that this seemed to be a very rum friend of Satterthwaite's. He glanced at him sideways. The fellow looked all right – quite a normal young chap. Rather dark, but not at all foreign-looking.

'And now,' said Satterthwaite importantly, 'I must tell you all about the case.'

He talked for some ten minutes. Sitting there in the darkness, rushing through the night, he had an intoxicating feeling of power. What did it matter if he were only a looker-on at life? He had words at his command, he was master of them, he could string them to a pattern – a strange Renaissance pattern composed of the beauty of Laura Dwighton, with her white arms and red hair – and the shadowy dark figure of Paul

Delangua, whom women found handsome.

Set that against the background of Alderway – Alderway that had stood since the days of Henry VII and, some said, before that. Alderway that was English to the core, with its clipped yew and its old beak barn and the fishpond, where monks had kept their carp for Fridays.

In a few deft strokes he had etched in Sir James, a Dwighton who was a true descendant of the old De Wittons, who long ago had wrung money out of the land and locked it fast in coffers, so that whoever else had fallen on evil days, the masters of Alderway had never become impoverished.

At last Mr Satterthwaite ceased. He was sure, had been sure all along, of the sympathy of his audience. He waited now the word of praise which was his due. It came.

'You are an artist, Mr Satterthwaite.'

'I – I do my best.' The little man was suddenly humble.

They had turned in at the lodge gates some minutes ago. Now the car drew up in front of the doorway, and a police constable came hurriedly down the steps to meet them.

'Good evening, sir. Inspector Curtis is in the library.'

'Right.'

Melrose ran up the steps followed by the other two.

As the three of them passed across the wide hall, an elderly butler peered from a doorway apprehensively. Melrose nodded to him.

'Evening, Miles. This is a sad business.'

'It is indeed,' the other quavered. 'I can hardly believe it, sir; indeed I can't. To think that anyone should strike down the master.'

'Yes, yes,' said Melrose, cutting him short. 'I'll have a talk with you presently.'

He strode on to the library. There a big, soldierly-looking inspector greeted him with respect.

'Nasty business, sir. I have not disturbed things. No fingerprints on the weapon. Whoever did it knew his business.'

Mr Satterthwaite looked at the bowed figure sitting at the big writing table, and looked hurriedly away again. The man had been struck down from behind, a smashing blow that had crashed in the skull. The sight was not a pretty one.

The weapon lay on the floor – a bronze figure about two feet high, the base of it stained and wet. Mr Satterthwaite bent over it curiously.

'A Venus,' he said softly. 'So he was struck down by Venus.'

He found food for poetic meditation in the thought.

'The windows,' said the inspector, 'were all closed and bolted on the inside.'

He paused significantly.

'Making an inside job of it,' said the chief constable reluctantly. 'Well – well, we'll see.'

The murdered man was dressed in golf clothes, and a bag of golf clubs had been flung untidily across a big leather couch.

'Just come in from the links,' explained the inspector, following the chief constable's glance. 'At five-fifteen, that was. Had tea brought here by the butler. Later he rang for his valet to bring him down a pair of soft slippers. As far as we can tell, the valet was the last person to see him alive.'

Melrose nodded, and turned his attention once more to the writing table.

A good many of the ornaments had been overturned and broken. Prominent among these was a big dark enamel clock, which lay on its side in the very centre of the table.

The inspector cleared his throat.

'That's what you might call a piece of luck, sir,' he said. 'As you see, it's stopped. *At half past six.* That gives us the time of the crime. Very convenient.'

The colonel was staring at the clock.

'As you say,' he remarked. 'Very convenient.' He paused a minute, and then added, 'Too damned convenient! I don't like it, Inspector.'

He looked around at the other two. His eye sought

Mr Quin's with a look of appeal in it.

'Damn it all,' he said. 'It's too neat. You know what I mean. Things don't happen like that.'

'You mean,' murmured Mr Quin, 'that clocks don't fall like that?'

Melrose stared at him for a moment, then back at the clock, which had that pathetic and innocent look familiar to objects which have been suddenly bereft of their dignity. Very carefully Colonel Melrose replaced it on its legs again. He struck the table a violent blow. The clock rocked, but it did not fall. Melrose repeated the action, and very slowly, with a kind of unwillingness, the clock fell over on its back.

'What time was the crime discovered?' demanded Melrose sharply.

'Just about seven o'clock, sir.'

'Who discovered it?'

'The butler.'

'Fetch him in,' said the chief constable. 'I'll see him now. Where is Lady Dwighton, by the way?'

'Lying down, sir. Her maid says that she's prostrated and can't see anyone.'

Melrose nodded, and Inspector Curtis went in search of the butler. Mr Quin was looking thoughtfully into the fireplace. Mr Satterthwaite followed his example. He blinked at the smouldering logs for a minute or two, and then something bright lying in the grate caught his eye. He stooped and picked up a little sliver of curved glass.

'You wanted me, sir?'

It was the butler's voice, still quavering and uncertain. Mr Satterthwaite slipped the fragment of glass into his waistcoat pocket and turned round.

The old man was standing in the doorway.

'Sit down,' said the chief constable kindly. 'You're shaking all over. It's been a shock to you, I expect.'

'It has indeed, sir.'

'Well, I shan't keep you long. Your master came in just after five, I believe?'

'Yes, sir. He ordered tea to be brought to him here. Afterward, when I came to take it away, he asked for Jennings to be sent to him – that's his valet, sir.'

'What time was that?'

'About ten minutes past six, sir.'

'Yes – well?'

'I sent word to Jennings, sir. And it wasn't till I came in here to shut the windows and draw the curtains at seven o'clock that I saw –'

Melrose cut him short. 'Yes, yes, you needn't go into all that. You didn't touch the body, or disturb anything, did you?'

'Oh! No indeed, sir! I went as fast as I could go to the telephone to ring up the police.'

'And then?'

'I told Jane – her ladyship's maid, sir – to break the news to her ladyship.'

'You haven't seen your mistress at all this evening?'

Colonel Melrose put the question casually enough, but Mr Satterthwaite's keen ears caught anxiety behind the words.

'Not to speak to, sir. Her ladyship has remained in her own apartments since the tragedy.'

'Did you see her before?'

The question came sharply, and everyone in the room noted the hesitation before the butler replied.

'I – I just caught a glimpse of her, sir, descending the staircase.'

'Did she come in here?'

Mr Satterthwaite held his breath.

'I – I think so, sir.'

'What time was that?'

You might have heard a pin drop. Did the old man know, Mr Satterthwaite wondered, what hung on his answer?

'It was just upon half past six, sir.'

Colonel Melrose drew a deep breath. 'That will do, thank you. Just send Jennings, the valet, to me, will you?'

Jennings answered the summons with promptitude. A narrow-faced man with a catlike tread. Something sly and secretive about him.

A man, thought Mr Satterthwaite, who would easily murder his master if he could be sure of not being found out.

He listened eagerly to the man's answers to Colonel Melrose's questions. But his story seemed straightforward enough. He had brought his master down some soft hide slippers and removed the brogues.

'What did you do after that, Jennings?'

'I went back to the stewards' room, sir.'

'At what time did you leave your master?'

'It must have been just after a quarter past six, sir.'

'Where were you at half past six, Jennings?'

'In the stewards' room, sir.'

Colonel Melrose dismissed the man with a nod. He looked across at Curtis inquiringly.

'Quite correct, sir, I checked that up. He was in the stewards' room from about six-twenty until seven o'clock.'

'Then that lets him out,' said the chief constable a trifle regretfully. 'Besides, there's no motive.'

They looked at each other.

There was a tap at the door.

'Come in,' said the colonel.

A scared-looking lady's maid appeared.

'If you please, her ladyship has heard that Colonel Melrose is here and she would like to see him.'

'Certainly,' said Melrose. 'I'll come at once. Will you show me the way?'

But a hand pushed the girl aside. A very different figure now stood in the doorway. Laura Dwighton looked like a visitor from another world.

She was dressed in a clinging medieval tea gown of dull blue brocade. Her auburn hair was parted in the middle and brought down over her ears. Conscious of the fact she had a style of her own, Lady Dwighton had never had her hair cut. It was drawn back into a simple knot on the nape of her neck. Her arms were bare.

One of them was outstretched to steady herself against the frame of the doorway, the other hung down by her side, clasping a book. *She looks*, Mr Satterthwaite thought, *like a Madonna from an early Italian canvas*.

She stood there, swaying slightly from side to side. Colonel Melrose sprang toward her.

'I've come to tell you – to tell you –'

Her voice was low and rich. Mr Satterthwaite was so entranced with the dramatic value of the scene that he had forgotten its reality.

'Please, Lady Dwighton –' Melrose had an arm round her, supporting her. He took her across the hall into a small anteroom, its walls hung with faded silk. Quin and Satterthwaite followed. She sank down on the low settee, her head resting back on a rust-coloured cushion, her eyelids closed. The three men watched her. Suddenly she opened her eyes and sat up. She spoke very quietly.

'*I killed him,*' she said. 'That's what I came to tell you. *I killed him!*'

There was a moment's agonized silence. Mr Satterthwaite's heart missed a beat.

'Lady Dwighton,' said Melrose. 'You've had a great shock – you're unstrung. I don't think you quite know what you're saying.'

Would she draw back now – while there was yet time?

'I know perfectly what I'm saying. It was I who shot him.'

Two of the men in the room gasped, the other made no sound. Laura Dwighton leaned still farther forward.

'Don't you understand? I came down and shot him. I admit it.'

The book she had been holding in her hand clattered to the floor. There was a paper cutter in it, a thing shaped like a dagger with a jewelled hilt. Mr Satterthwaite picked it up mechanically and placed it on the table. As he did so he thought, *That's a dangerous toy. You could kill a man with that.*

'Well –' Laura Dwighton's voice was impatient. '– what are you going to do about it? Arrest me? Take me away?'

Colonel Melrose found his voice with difficulty.

'What you have told me is very serious, Lady Dwighton. I must ask you to go to your room till I have – er – made arrangements.'

She nodded and rose to her feet. She was quite composed now, grave and cold.

As she turned toward the door, Mr Quin spoke. 'What did you do with the revolver, Lady Dwighton?'

A flicker of uncertainty passed across her face. 'I – I dropped it there on the floor. No, I think I threw it out of the window – oh! I can't remember now. What does it matter? I hardly knew what I was doing. It doesn't matter, does it?'

'No,' said Mr Quin. 'I hardly think it matters.'

She looked at him in perplexity with a shade of something that might have been alarm. Then she flung back her head and went imperiously out of the room. Mr Satterthwaite hastened after her. She might, he felt, collapse at any minute. But she was already halfway up the staircase, displaying no sign of her earlier weakness. The scared-looking maid was standing at the foot of the stairway, and Mr Satterthwaite spoke to her authoritatively.

'Look after your mistress,' he said.

'Yes, sir.' The girl prepared to ascend after the blue-robed figure. 'Oh, please, sir, they don't suspect him, do they?'

'Suspect whom?'

'Jennings, sir. Oh! Indeed, sir, he wouldn't hurt a fly.'

'Jennings? No, of course not. Go and look after your mistress.'

'Yes, sir.'

The girl ran quickly up the staircase. Mr Satterthwaite returned to the room he had just vacated.

Colonel Melrose was saying heavily, 'Well, I'm jiggered. There's more in this than meets the eye. It – it's like those dashed silly things heroines do in many novels.'

'It's unreal,' agreed Mr Satterthwaite. 'It's like something on the stage.'

Mr Quin nodded. 'Yes, you admire the drama, do you not? You are a man who appreciates good acting when you see it.'

Mr Satterthwaite looked hard at him.

In the silence that followed a far-off sound came to their ears.

'Sounds like a shot,' said Colonel Melrose. 'One of the keepers, I daresay. That's probably what she heard. Perhaps she went down to see. She wouldn't go close or examine the body. She'd leap at once to the conclusion –'

'Mr Delangua, sir.' It was the old butler who spoke, standing apologetically in the doorway.

'Eh?' said Melrose. 'What's that?'

'Mr Delangua is here, sir, and would like to speak to you if he may.'

Colonel Melrose leaned back in his chair. 'Show him in,' he said grimly.

A moment later Paul Delangua stood in the doorway. As Colonel Melrose had hinted, there was something un-English about him – the easy grace of his movements, the dark, handsome face, the eyes set a little too near together. There hung about him the air of the Renaissance. He and Laura Dwighton suggested the same atmosphere.

'Good evening, gentlemen,' said Delangua. He made a little theatrical bow.

'I don't know what your business may be, Mr Delangua,' said Colonel Melrose sharply, 'but if it is nothing to do with the matter at hand –'

Delangua interrupted him with a laugh. 'On the contrary,' he said, 'it has everything to do with it.'

'What do you mean?'

'I mean,' said Delangua quietly, 'that I have come to give myself up for the murder of Sir James Dwighton.'

'You know what you are saying?' said Melrose gravely.

'Perfectly.'

The young man's eyes were riveted to the table.

'I don't understand –'

'Why I give myself up? Call it remorse – call it anything you please. I stabbed him, right enough – you may be quite sure of that.' He nodded toward the table. 'You've got the weapon there, I see. A very handy little tool. Lady Dwighton unfortunately left it lying around in a book, and I happened to snatch it up.'

'One minute,' said Colonel Melrose. 'Am I to understand that you admit stabbing Sir James with this?' He held the dagger aloft.

'Quite right. I stole in through the window, you know. He had his back to me. It was quite easy. I left the same way.'

'Through the window?'

'Through the window, of course.'

'And what time was this?'

Delangua hesitated. 'Let me see – I was talking to the keeper fellow – that was at a quarter past six. I heard the church tower chime. It must have been – well, say somewhere about half past.'

A grim smile came to the colonel's lips.

'Quite right, young man,' he said. 'Half past six was the time. Perhaps you've heard that already? But this is altogether a most peculiar murder!'

'Why?'

'So many people confess to it,' said Colonel Melrose.

They heard the sharp intake of the other's breath.

'Who else has confessed to it?' he asked in a voice that he vainly strove to render steady.

'Lady Dwighton.'

Delangua threw back his head and laughed in rather a forced manner. 'Lady Dwighton is apt to be hysterical,' he said lightly. 'I shouldn't pay any attention to what she says if I were you.'

'I don't think I shall,' said Melrose. 'But there's another odd thing about this murder.'

'What's that?'

'Well,' said Melrose, 'Lady Dwighton has confessed to having shot Sir James, and you have confessed to having stabbed him. But luckily for both of you, he wasn't shot or stabbed, you see. His skull was smashed in.'

'My God!' cried Delangua. 'But a woman couldn't possibly do that –'

He stopped, biting his lip. Melrose nodded with the ghost of a smile.

'Often read of it,' he volunteered. 'Never seen it happen.'

'What?'

'Couple of young idiots each accusing themselves because they thought the other had done it,' said Melrose. 'Now we've got to begin at the beginning.'

'The valet,' cried Mr Satterthwaite. 'That girl just now – I wasn't paying any attention at the time.' He paused, striving for coherence. 'She was afraid of our suspecting him. There must be some motive that he had and which we don't know, but she does.'

Colonel Melrose frowned, then he rang the bell. When it was answered, he said, 'Please ask Lady Dwighton if she will be good enough to come down again.'

They waited in silence until she came. At sight of Delangua she started and stretched out a hand to save herself from falling. Colonel Melrose came quickly to the rescue.

'It's quite all right, Lady Dwighton. Please don't be alarmed.'

'I don't understand. What is Mr Delangua doing here?'

Delangua came over to her, 'Laura – Laura – why did you do it?'

'Do it?'

'I know. It was for me – because you thought that – After all, it was natural, I suppose. But, oh! You angel!'

Colonel Melrose cleared his throat. He was a man who disliked emotion and had a horror of anything approaching a 'scene'.

'If you'll allow me to say so, Lady Dwighton, both you and Mr Delangua have had a lucky escape. He had just arrived in his turn to "confess" to the murder – oh, it's quite all right, he didn't do it! But what we want to know is the truth. No more shillyshallying. The butler says you went into the library at half past six – is that so?'

Laura looked at Delangua. He nodded.

'The truth, Laura,' he said. 'That is what we want now.'

She breathed a deep sigh. 'I will tell you.'

She sank down on a chair that Mr Satterthwaite had hurriedly pushed forward.

'I did come down. I opened the library door and I saw –'

She stopped and swallowed. Mr Satterthwaite leaned forward and patted her hand encouragingly.

'Yes,' he said. 'Yes. You saw?'

'My husband was lying across the writing table. I saw his head – the blood – oh!'

She put her hands to her face. The chief constable leaned forward.

'Excuse me, Lady Dwighton. You thought Mr Delangua had shot him?'

She nodded. 'Forgive me, Paul,' she pleaded. 'But you said – you said –'

'That I'd shoot him like a dog,' said Delangua grimly. 'I remember. That was the day I discovered he'd been ill-treating you.'

The chief constable kept sternly to the matter in hand.

'Then I am to understand, Lady Dwighton, that you went upstairs again and – er – said nothing. We needn't go into your reason. You didn't touch the body or go near the writing table?'

She shuddered.

'No, no. I ran straight out of the room.'

'I see, I see. And what time was this exactly? Do you know?'

'It was just half past six when I got back to my bedroom.'

'Then at – say five-and-twenty past six, Sir James was already dead.' The chief constable looked at the others. 'That clock – it was faked, eh? We suspected that all along. Nothing easier than to move the hands to whatever time you wished, but they made a mistake to lay it down on its side like that. Well, that seems to narrow it down to the butler or the valet, and I can't believe it's the butler. Tell me, Lady Dwighton, did this man Jennings have any grudge against your husband?'

Laura lifted her face from her hands. 'Not exactly a grudge, but – well, James told me only this morning that he'd dismissed him. He'd found him pilfering.'

'Ah! Now we're getting at it. Jennings would have been dismissed without a character. A serious matter for him.'

'You said something about a clock,' said Laura

Dwighton. 'There's just a chance – if you want to fix the time – James would have been sure to have his little golf watch on him. Mightn't that have been smashed, too, when he fell forward?'

'It's an idea,' said the colonel slowly. 'But I'm afraid – Curtis!'

The inspector nodded in quick comprehension and left the room. He returned a minute later. On the palm of his hand was a silver watch marked like a golf ball, the kind that are sold for golfers to carry loose in a pocket with balls.

'Here it is, sir,' he said, 'but I doubt if it will be any good. They're tough, these watches.'

The colonel took it from him and held it to his ear.

'It seems to have stopped, anyway,' he observed.

He pressed with his thumb, and the lid of the watch flew open. Inside the glass was cracked across.

'Ah!' he said exultantly.

The hand pointed to exactly a quarter past six.

II

'A very good glass of port, Colonel Melrose,' said Mr Quin.

It was half past nine, and the three men had just

finished a belated dinner at Colonel Melrose's house. Mr Satterthwaite was particularly jubilant.

'I was quite right,' he chuckled. 'You can't deny it, Mr Quin. You turned up tonight to save two absurd young people who were both bent on putting their heads into a noose.'

'Did I?' said Mr Quin. 'Surely not. I did nothing at all.'

'As it turned out, it was not necessary,' agreed Mr Satterthwaite. 'But it might have been. It was touch and go, you know. I shall never forget the moment when Lady Dwighton said, "I killed him." I've never seen anything on the stage half as dramatic.'

'I'm inclined to agree with you,' said Mr Quin.

'Wouldn't have believed such a thing could happen outside a novel,' declared the colonel, for perhaps the twentieth time that night.

'Does it?' asked Mr Quin.

The colonel stared at him, 'Damn it, it happened tonight.'

'Mind you,' interposed Mr Satterthwaite, leaning back and sipping his port, 'Lady Dwighton was magnificent, quite magnificent, but she made one mistake. She shouldn't have leaped to the conclusion that her husband had been shot. In the same way Delangua was a fool to assume that he had been stabbed just because the dagger happened to be lying on the table in front of us. It was a mere coincidence that Lady Dwighton should have brought it down with her.'

'Was it?' asked Mr Quin.

'Now if they'd only confined themselves to saying that they'd killed Sir James, without particularizing how –' went on Mr Satterthwaite – 'what would have been the result?'

'They might have been believed,' said Mr Quin with an odd smile.

'The whole thing was exactly like a novel,' said the colonel.

'That's where they got the idea from, I daresay,' said Mr Quin.

'Possibly,' agreed Mr Satterthwaite. 'Things one has read do come back to one in the oddest way.' He looked across at Mr Quin. 'Of course,' he said, 'the clock really looked suspicious from the first. One ought never to forget how easy it is to put the hands of a clock or watch forward or back.'

Mr Quin nodded and repeated the words. 'Forward,' he said, and paused. 'Or back.'

There was something encouraging in his voice. His bright, dark eyes were fixed on Mr Satterthwaite.

'The hands of the clock were put forward,' said Mr Satterthwaite. 'We know that.'

'Were they?' asked Mr Quin.

Mr Satterthwaite stared at him. 'Do you mean,' he

said slowly, 'that it was the watch which was put back? But that doesn't make sense. It's impossible.'

'Not impossible,' murmured Mr Quin.

'Well – absurd. To whose advantage could that be?'

'Only, I suppose, to someone who had an *alibi* for that time.'

'By gad!' cried the colonel. 'That's the time young Delangua said he was talking to the keeper.'

'He told us that very particularly,' said Mr Satterthwaite.

They looked at each other. They had an uneasy feeling as of solid ground failing beneath their feet. Facts went spinning round, turning new and unexpected faces. And in the centre of the kaleidoscope was the dark, smiling face of Mr Quin.

'But in that case –' began Melrose '– in that case –'

Mr Satterthwaite, nimble-witted, finished his sentence for him. 'It's all the other way round. A plant just the same – but a plant against the valet. Oh, but it can't be! It's impossible. Why each of them accused themselves of the crime.'

'Yes,' said Mr Quin. 'Up till then you suspected them, didn't you?' His voice went on, placid and dreamy. 'Just like something out of a book, you said, colonel. They got the idea there. It's what the innocent hero and heroine do. Of course it made you think them innocent – there was the force of tradition behind them.

Mr Satterthwaite has been saying all along it was like something on the stage. You were both right. It wasn't real. You've been saying so all along without knowing what you were saying. They'd have told a much better story than that if they'd wanted to be believed.'

The two men looked at him helplessly.

'It would be clever,' said Mr Satterthwaite slowly. 'It would be diabolically clever. And I've thought of something else. The butler said he went in at seven to shut the windows – so he must have expected them to be open.'

'That's the way Delangua came in,' said Mr Quin. 'He killed Sir James with one blow, and he and she together did what they had to do –'

He looked at Mr Satterthwaite, encouraging him to reconstruct the scene. He did so, hesitatingly.

'They smashed the clock and put it on its side. Yes. They altered the watch and smashed it. Then he went out of the window, and she fastened it after him. But there's one thing I don't see. Why bother with the watch at all? Why not simply put back the hands of the clock?'

'The clock was always a little obvious,' said Mr Quin. 'Anyone might have seen through a rather transparent device like that.'

'But surely the watch was too far-fetched. Why, it was pure chance that we ever thought of the watch.'

'Oh, no,' said Mr Quin. 'It was the lady's suggestion, remember.'

Mr Satterthwaite stared at him, fascinated.

'And yet, you know,' said Mr Quin dreamily, 'the one person who wouldn't be likely to overlook the watch would be the valet. Valets know better than anyone what their masters carry in their pockets. If he altered the clock, the valet would have altered the watch, too. They don't understand human nature, those two. They are not like Mr Satterthwaite.'

Mr Satterthwaite shook his head.

'I was all wrong,' he murmured humbly. 'I thought that you had come to save them.'

'So I did,' said Mr Quin. 'Oh! Not those two – the others. Perhaps you didn't notice the lady's maid? She wasn't wearing blue brocade, or acting a dramatic part. But she's really a very pretty girl, and I think she loves that man Jennings very much. I think that between you you'll be able to save her man from getting hanged.'

'We've no proof of any kind,' said Colonel Melrose heavily.

Mr Quin smiled. 'Mr Satterthwaite has.'

'I?' Mr Satterthwaite was astonished.

Mr Quin went on. 'You've got a proof that that watch wasn't smashed in Sir James's pocket. You can't smash a watch like that without opening the case. Just try it and see. Someone took the watch out and opened it, set back the hands, smashed the glass, and then shut it and put it back. They never noticed that a fragment of glass was missing.'

'Oh!' cried Mr Satterthwaite. His hand flew to his waistcoat pocket. He drew out a fragment of curved glass.

It was his moment.

'With this,' said Mr Satterthwaite importantly, 'I shall save a man from death.'

Next to a Dog

I

The ladylike woman behind the Registry Office table cleared her throat and peered across at the girl who sat opposite.

'Then you refuse to consider the post? It only came in this morning. A very nice part of Italy, I believe, a widower with a little boy of three and an elderly lady, his mother or aunt.'

Joyce Lambert shook her head.

'I can't go out of England,' she said in a tired voice; 'there are reasons. If only you could find me a daily post?'

Her voice shook slightly – ever so slightly, for she had it well under control. Her dark blue eyes looked appealingly at the woman opposite her.

'It's very difficult, Mrs Lambert. The only kind of daily governess required is one who has full qualifications. You have none. I have hundreds on my books

– literally hundreds.' She paused. 'You have someone at home you can't leave?'

Joyce nodded.

'A child?'

'No, not a child.' And a faint smile flickered across her face.

'Well, it is very unfortunate. I will do my best, of course, but –'

The interview was clearly at an end. Joyce rose. She was biting her lip to keep the tears from springing to her eyes as she emerged from the frowsy office into the street.

'You mustn't,' she admonished herself sternly. 'Don't be a snivelling little idiot. You're panicking – that's what you're doing – panicking. No good ever came of giving way to panic. It's quite early in the day still and lots of things may happen. Aunt Mary ought to be good for a fortnight anyway. Come on, girl, step out, and don't keep your well-to-do relations waiting.'

She walked down Edgware Road, across the park, and then down to Victoria Street, where she turned into the Army and Navy Stores. She went to the lounge and sat down glancing at her watch. It was just half past one. Five minutes sped by and then an elderly lady with her arms full of parcels bore down upon her.

'Ah! There you are, Joyce. I'm a few minutes late, I'm afraid. The service is not as good as it used to be in the luncheon room. You've had lunch, of course?'

Joyce hesitated a minute or two, then she said quietly: 'Yes, thank you.'

'I always have mine at half past twelve,' said Aunt Mary, settling herself comfortably with her parcels. 'Less rush and a clearer atmosphere. The curried eggs here are excellent.'

'Are they?' said Joyce faintly. She felt that she could hardly bear to think of curried eggs – the hot steam rising from them – the delicious smell! She wrenched her thoughts resolutely aside.

'You look peaky, child,' said Aunt Mary, who was herself of a comfortable figure. 'Don't go in for this modern fad of eating no meat. All fal-de-lal. A good slice off the joint never did anyone any harm.'

Joyce stopped herself from saying, 'It wouldn't do me any harm now.' If only Aunt Mary would stop talking about food. To raise your hopes by asking you to meet her at half past one and then to talk of curried eggs and slices of roast meat – oh! cruel – cruel.

'Well, my dear,' said Aunt Mary. 'I got your letter – and it was very nice of you to take me at my word. I said I'd be pleased to see you anytime and so I should have been – but as it happens, I've just had an extremely good offer to let the house. Quite too good to be missed, and bringing their own plate and linen. Five months. They come in on Thursday and I go to Harrogate. My rheumatism's been troubling me lately.'

'I see,' said Joyce. 'I'm so sorry.'

'So it'll have to be for another time. Always pleased to see you, my dear.'

'Thank you, Aunt Mary.'

'You know, you do look peaky,' said Aunt Mary, considering her attentively. 'You're thin, too; no flesh on your bones, and what's happened to your pretty colour? You always had a nice healthy colour. Mind you take plenty of exercise.'

'I'm taking plenty of exercise today,' said Joyce grimly. She rose. 'Well Aunt Mary, I must be getting along.'

Back again – through St James's Park this time, and so on through Berkeley Square and across Oxford Street and up Edgware Road, past Praed Street to the point where the Edgware Road begins to think of becoming something else. Then aside, through a series of dirty little streets till one particular dingy house was reached.

Joyce inserted her latchkey and entered a small frowsy hall. She ran up the stairs till she reached the top landing. A door faced her and from the bottom of this door a snuffling noise proceeded succeeded in a second by a series of joyful whines and yelps.

'Yes, Terry darling – it's Missus come home.'

As the door opened, a white body precipitated itself upon the girl – an aged wire-haired terrier very shaggy as to coat and suspiciously bleary as to eyes. Joyce gathered him up in her arms and sat down on the floor.

'Terry darling! Darling, darling Terry. Love your Missus, Terry; love your Missus a lot!'

And Terry obeyed, his eager tongue worked busily, he licked her face, her ears, her neck and all the time his stump of a tail wagged furiously.

'Terry darling, what are we going to do? What's going to become of us? Oh! Terry darling, I'm so tired.'

'Now then, miss,' said a tart voice behind her. 'If you'll give over hugging and kissing that dog, here's a cup of nice hot tea for you.'

'Oh! Mrs Barnes, how good of you.'

Joyce scrambled to her feet. Mrs Barnes was a big, formidable-looking woman. Beneath the exterior of a dragon she concealed an unexpectedly warm heart.

'A cup of hot tea never did anyone any harm,' enunciated Mrs Barnes, voicing the universal sentiment of her class.

Joyce sipped gratefully. Her landlady eyed her covertly.

'Any luck, miss – ma'am, I should say?'

Joyce shook her head, her face clouded over.

'Ah!' said Mrs Barnes with a sigh. 'Well, it doesn't seem to be what you might call a lucky day.'

Joyce looked up sharply.

'Oh, Mrs Barnes – you don't mean –'

Mrs Barnes was nodding gloomily.

'Yes – it's Barnes. Out of work again. What we're going to do, I'm sure I don't know.'

'Oh, Mrs Barnes – I must – I mean you'll want –'

'Now don't you fret, my dear. I'm not denying but that I'd be glad if you'd found something – but if you haven't – you haven't. Have you finished that tea? I'll take the cup.'

'Not quite.'

'Ah!' said Mrs Barnes accusingly. 'You're going to give what's left to that dratted dog – I know you.'

'Oh, please, Mrs Barnes. Just a little drop. You don't mind really, do you?'

'It wouldn't be any use if I did. You're crazy about that cantankerous brute. Yes, that's what I say – and that's what he is. As near as nothing bit me this morning, he did.'

'Oh, no, Mrs Barnes! Terry wouldn't do such a thing.'

'Growled at me – showed his teeth. I was just trying to see if there was anything could be done to those shoes of yours.'

'He doesn't like anyone touching my things. He thinks he ought to guard them.'

'Well, what does he want to think for? It isn't a dog's business to think. He'd be well enough in his proper place, tied up in the yard to keep off burglars. All this cuddling! He ought to be put away, miss – that's what I say.'

'No, no, no. Never. Never!'

'Please yourself,' said Mrs Barnes. She took the cup from the table, retrieved the saucer from the floor where Terry had just finished his share, and stalked from the room.

'Terry,' said Joyce. 'Come here and talk to me. What are we going to do, my sweet?'

She settled herself in the rickety armchair, with Terry on her knees. She threw off her hat and leaned back. She put one of Terry's paws on each side of her neck and kissed him lovingly on his nose and between his eyes. Then she began talking to him in a soft low voice, twisting his ears gently between her fingers.

'What are we going to do about Mrs Barnes, Terry? We owe her four weeks – and she's such a lamb, Terry – such a lamb. She'd never turn us out. But we can't take advantage of her being a lamb, Terry. We can't do that. Why does Barnes want to be out of work? I hate Barnes. He's always getting drunk. And if you're always getting drunk, you are usually out of work. But I don't get drunk, Terry, and yet I'm out of work.

'I can't leave you, darling. I can't leave you. There's not even anyone I could leave you with – nobody who'd be good to you. You're getting old, Terry – twelve years old – and nobody wants an old dog who's rather blind and a little deaf and a little – yes, just a little – bad-tempered. You're sweet to me, darling, but you're not sweet to everyone, are you? You growl. It's because you know the world's turning against you. We've just got each other, haven't we, darling?'

Terry licked her cheek delicately.

'Talk to me, darling.'

Terry gave a long lingering groan – almost a sigh, then he nuzzled his nose in behind Joyce's ear.

'You trust me, don't you, angel? You know I'd never leave you. But what are we going to do? We're right down to it now, Terry.'

She settled back further in the chair, her eyes half closed.

'Do you remember, Terry, all the happy times we used to have? You and I and Michael and Daddy. Oh, Michael – Michael! It was his first leave, and he wanted to give me a present before he went back to France. And I told him not to be extravagant.

And then we were down in the country – and it was all a surprise. He told me to look out of the window, and there you were, dancing up the path on a long lead. The funny little man who brought you, a little man who smelt of dogs. How he talked. "The goods, that's what he is. Look at him, ma'am, ain't he a picture? I said to myself, as soon as the lady and gentleman see him they'll say: 'That dog's the goods!'"

'He kept on saying that – and we called you that for quite a long time – the Goods! Oh, Terry, you were such a darling of a puppy, with your little head on one side, wagging your absurd tail! And Michael went away to France and I had you – the darlingest dog in the world. You read all Michael's letters with me, didn't you? You'd sniff them, and I'd say – "From Master," and you'd understand. We were so happy – so happy. You and Michael and I. And now Michael's dead, and you're old, and I – I'm so tired of being brave.'

Terry licked her.

'You were there when the telegram came. If it hadn't been for you, Terry – if I hadn't had you to hold on to . . .'

She stayed silent for some minutes.

'And we've been together ever since – been through all the ups and downs together – there have been a lot of downs, haven't there? And now we've come right up against it. There are only Michael's aunts, and they think I'm all right. They don't know he gambled that money away. We must never tell anyone that. *I* don't care – why shouldn't he? Everyone has to have some fault. He loved us both, Terry, and that's all that matters. His own relations were always inclined to be down on him and to say nasty things. We're not going to give them the chance. But I wish I had some relations of my own. It's very awkward having no relations at all.

'I'm so tired, Terry – and remarkably hungry. I can't believe I'm only twenty-nine – I feel sixty-nine. I'm not really brave – I only pretend to be. And I'm getting awfully mean ideas. I walked all the way to Ealing yesterday to see Cousin Charlotte Green. I thought if I got there at half past twelve she'd be sure to ask me to stop to lunch. And then when I got to the house, I felt it was too cadging for anything. I just couldn't. So I walked all the way back. And that's foolish. You should be a determined cadger or else not even think of it. I don't think I'm a strong character.'

Terry groaned again and put a black nose into Joyce's eye.

'You've got a lovely nose still, Terry – all cold like ice cream. Oh, I do love you so! I can't part from you.

I can't have you "put away", I can't . . . I can't . . . I can't . . .'

The warm tongue licked eagerly.

'You understand so, my sweet. You'd do anything to help Missus, wouldn't you?'

Terry clambered down and went unsteadily to a corner. He came back holding a battered bowl between his teeth.

Joyce was midway between tears and laughter.

'Was he doing his only trick? The only thing he could think of to help Missus. Oh, Terry – Terry – nobody shall part us! I'd do anything. Would I, though? One says that – and then when you're shown the thing, you say, "I didn't mean anything like *that.*" Would I do anything?'

She got down on the floor beside the dog.

'You see, Terry, it's like this. Nursery governesses can't have dogs, and companions to elderly ladies can't have dogs. Only married women can have dogs, Terry – little fluggy expensive dogs that they take shopping with them – and if one preferred an old blind terrier – well, why not?'

She stopped frowning and at that minute there was a double knock from below.

'The post. I wonder.'

She jumped up and hurried down the stairs, returning with a letter.

'It might be. If only . . .'

She tore it open.

Dear Madam,

We have inspected the picture and our opinion is that it is not a genuine Cuyp and that its value is practically nil.

Yours truly,

Sloane & Ryder

Joyce stood holding it. When she spoke, her voice had changed.

'That's that,' she said. 'The last hope gone. But we won't be parted. There's a way – and it won't be cadging. Terry darling, I'm going out. I'll be back soon.'

Joyce hurried down the stairs to where the telephone stood in a dark corner. There she asked for a certain number. A man's voice answered her, its tone changing as he realized her identity.

'Joyce, my dear girl. Come out and have some dinner and dance tonight.'

'I can't,' said Joyce lightly. 'Nothing fit to wear.'

And she smiled grimly as she thought of the empty pegs in the flimsy cupboard.

'How would it be if I came along and saw you now? What's the address? Good Lord, where's that? Rather come off your high horse, haven't you?'

'Completely.'

'Well, you're frank about it. So long.'

Arthur Halliday's car drew up outside the house about three quarters of an hour later. An awestruck Mrs Barnes conducted him upstairs.

'My dear girl – what an awful hole. What on earth has got you into this mess?'

'Pride and a few other unprofitable emotions.'

She spoke lightly enough; her eyes looked at the man opposite her sardonically.

Many people called Halliday handsome. He was a big man with square shoulders, fair, with small, very pale blue eyes and a heavy chin.

He sat down on the rickety chair she indicated.

'Well,' he said thoughtfully. 'I should say you'd had your lesson. I say – will that brute bite?'

'No, no, he's all right. I've trained him to be rather a – a watchdog.'

Halliday was looking her up and down.

'Going to climb down, Joyce,' he said softly. 'Is that it?'

Joyce nodded.

'I told you before, my dear girl. I always get what I want in the end. I knew you'd come in time to see which way your bread was buttered.'

'It's lucky for me you haven't changed your mind,' said Joyce.

He looked at her suspiciously. With Joyce you never knew quite what she was driving at.

'You'll marry me?'

She nodded. 'As soon as you please.'

'The sooner, the better, in fact.' He laughed, looking round the room. Joyce flushed.

'By the way, there's a condition.'

'A condition?' He looked suspicious again.

'My dog. He must come with me.'

'This old scarecrow? You can have any kind of a dog you choose. Don't spare expense.'

'I want Terry.'

'Oh! All right, please yourself.'

Joyce was staring at him.

'You do know – don't you – that I don't love you? Not in the least.'

'I'm not worrying about that. I'm not thin-skinned. But no hanky-panky, my girl. If you marry me, you play fair.'

The colour flashed into Joyce's cheeks.

'You will have your money's worth,' she said.

'What about a kiss now?'

He advanced upon her. She waited, smiling. He took her in his arms, kissing her face, her lips, her neck. She neither stiffened nor drew back. He released her at last.

'I'll get you a ring,' he said. 'What would you like, diamonds or pearls?'

'A ruby,' said Joyce. 'The largest ruby possible – the colour of blood.'

'That's an odd idea.'

'I should like it to be a contrast to the little half hoop of pearls that was all that Michael could afford to give me.'

'Better luck this time, eh?'

'You put things wonderfully, Arthur.'

Halliday went out chuckling.

'Terry,' said Joyce. 'Lick me – lick hard – all over my face and my neck – particularly my neck.'

And as Terry obeyed, she murmured reflectively:

'Thinking of something else very hard – that's the only way. You'd never guess what I thought of – jam – jam in a grocer's shop. I said it over to myself. Strawberry, blackcurrant, raspberry, damson. And perhaps, Terry, he'll get tired of me fairly soon. I hope so, don't you? They say men do when they're married to you. But Michael wouldn't have tired of me – never – never – never – Oh! Michael . . .'

II

Joyce rose the next morning with a heart like lead. She gave a deep sigh and immediately Terry, who slept on her bed, had moved up and was kissing her affectionately.

'Oh, darling – darling! We've got to go through with it. But if only something would happen. Terry darling, can't you help Missus? You would if you could, I know.'

Mrs Barnes brought up some tea and bread and butter and was heartily congratulatory.

'There now, ma'am, to think of you going to marry that gentleman. It was a Rolls he came in. It was indeed. It quite sobered Barnes up to think of one of them Rolls standing outside our door. Why, I declare that dog's sitting out on the window sill.'

'He likes the sun,' said Joyce. 'But it's rather dangerous. Terry, come in.'

'I'd have the poor dear put out of his misery if I was you,' said Mrs Barnes, 'and get your gentleman to buy you one of them plumy dogs as ladies carry in their muffs.'

Joyce smiled and called again to Terry. The dog rose awkwardly and just at that moment the noise of a dog fight rose from the street below. Terry craned his neck forward and added some brisk barking. The window sill was old and rotten. It tilted and Terry, too old and stiff to regain his balance, fell.

With a wild cry, Joyce ran down the stairs and out of the front door. In a few seconds she was kneeling by Terry's side. He was whining pitifully and his position showed her that he was badly hurt. She bent over him.

'Terry – Terry darling – darling, darling, darling –'

Very feebly, he tried to wag his tail.

'Terry boy – Missus will make you better – darling boy –'

A crowd, mainly composed of small boys, was pushing round.

'Fell from the window, 'e did.'

'My, 'e looks bad.'

'Broke 'is back as likely as not.'

Joyce paid no heed.

'Mrs Barnes, where's the nearest vet?'

'There's Jobling – round in Mere Street – if you could get him there.'

'A taxi.'

'Allow me.'

It was the pleasant voice of an elderly man who had just alighted from a taxi. He knelt down by Terry and lifted the upper lip, then passed his hand down the dog's body.

'I'm afraid he may be bleeding internally,' he said. 'There don't seem to be any bones broken. We'd better get him along to the vet's.'

Between them, he and Joyce lifted the dog. Terry gave a yelp of pain. His teeth met in Joyce's arm.

'Terry – it's all right – all right, old man.'

They got him into the taxi and drove off. Joyce wrapped a handkerchief round her arm in an absent-minded way. Terry, distressed, tried to lick it.

'I know, darling; I know. You didn't mean to hurt me. It's all right. It's all right, Terry.'

She stroked his head. The man opposite watched her but said nothing.

They arrived at the vet's fairly quickly and found him in. He was a red-faced man with an unsympathetic manner.

He handled Terry none too gently while Joyce stood by, agonized. The tears were running down her face. She kept on talking in a low, reassuring voice.

'It's all right, darling. It's all right . . .'

The vet straightened himself.

'Impossible to say exactly. I must make a proper examination. You must leave him here.'

'Oh! I can't.'

'I'm afraid you must. I must take him below. I'll telephone you in – say – half an hour.'

Sick at heart, Joyce gave in. She kissed Terry on his

nose. Blind with tears, she stumbled down the steps. The man who had helped her was still there. She had forgotten him.

'The taxi's still here. I'll take you back.' She shook her head.

'I'd rather walk.'

'I'll walk with you.'

He paid off the taxi. She was hardly conscious of him as he walked quietly by her side without speaking. When they arrived at Mrs Barnes', he spoke.

'Your wrist. You must see to it.'

She looked down at it.

'Oh! That's all right.'

'It wants properly washing and tying up. I'll come in with you.'

He went with her up the stairs. She let him wash the place and bind it up with a clean handkerchief. She only said one thing.

'Terry didn't mean to do it. He would never, *never* mean to do it. He just didn't realize it was me. He must have been in dreadful pain.'

'I'm afraid so, yes.'

'And perhaps they're hurting him dreadfully now?'

'I'm sure that everything that can be done for him is being done. When the vet rings up, you can go and get him and nurse him here.'

'Yes, of course.'

The man paused, then moved towards the door.

'I hope it will be all right,' he said awkwardly. 'Goodbye.'

'Goodbye.'

Two or three minutes later it occurred to her that he had been kind and that she had never thanked him.

Mrs Barnes appeared, cup in hand.

'Now, my poor lamb, a cup of hot tea. You're all to pieces, I can see that.'

'Thank you, Mrs Barnes, but I don't want any tea.'

'It would do you good, dearie. Don't take on so now. The doggie will be all right and even if he isn't that gentleman of yours will give you a pretty new dog –'

'Don't, Mrs Barnes. Don't. Please, if you don't mind, I'd rather be left alone.'

'Well, I never – there's the telephone.'

Joyce sped down to it like an arrow. She lifted the receiver. Mrs Barnes panted down after her. She heard Joyce say, 'Yes – speaking. What? Oh! Oh! Yes. Yes, thank you.'

She put back the receiver. The face she turned to Mrs Barnes startled that good woman. It seemed devoid of any life or expression.

'Terry's dead, Mrs Barnes,' she said. 'He died alone there without me.'

She went upstairs and, going into her room, shut the door very decisively.

'Well, I never,' said Mrs Barnes to the hall wallpaper.

Five minutes later she poked her head into the room. Joyce was sitting bolt upright in a chair. She was not crying.

'It's your gentleman, miss. Shall I send him up?'

A sudden light came into Joyce's eyes.

'Yes, please. I'd like to see him.'

Halliday came in boisterously.

'Well, here we are. I haven't lost much time, have I? I'm prepared to carry you off from this dreadful place here and now. You can't stay here. Come on, get your things on.'

'There's no need, Arthur.'

'No need? What do you mean?'

'Terry's dead. I don't need to marry you now.'

'What are you talking about?'

'My dog – Terry. He's dead. I was only marrying you so that we could be together.'

Halliday stared at her, his face growing redder and redder. 'You're mad.'

'I dare say. People who love dogs are.'

'You seriously tell me that you were only marrying me because – Oh, it's absurd!'

'Why did you think I was marrying you? You knew I hated you.'

'You were marrying me because I could give you a jolly good time – and so I can.'

'To my mind,' said Joyce, 'that is a much more revolting motive than mine. Anyway, it's off. I'm not marrying you!'

'Do you realize that you are treating me damned badly?'

She looked at him coolly but with such a blaze in her eyes that he drew back before it.

'I don't think so. I've heard you talk about getting a kick out of life. That's what you got out of me – and my dislike of you heightened it. You knew I hated you and you enjoyed it. When I let you kiss me yesterday, you were disappointed because I didn't flinch or wince. There's something brutal in you, Arthur, something cruel – something that likes hurting . . . Nobody could treat you as badly as you deserve. And now do you mind getting out of my room? I want it to myself.'

He spluttered a little.

'Wh – what are you going to do? You've no money.'

'That's my business. Please go.'

'You little devil. You absolutely maddening little devil. You haven't done with me yet.'

Joyce laughed.

The laugh routed him as nothing else had done. It was so unexpected. He went awkwardly down the stairs and drove away.

Joyce heaved a sigh. She pulled on her shabby black

felt hat and in her turn went out. She walked along the streets mechanically, neither thinking nor feeling. Somewhere at the back of her mind there was pain – pain that she would presently feel, but for the moment everything was mercifully dulled.

She passed the Registry Office and hesitated.

'I must do something. There's the river, of course. I've often thought of that. Just finish everything. But it's so cold and wet. I don't think I'm brave enough. I'm not brave really.'

She turned into the Registry Office.

'Good morning, Mrs Lambert. I'm afraid we've no daily post.'

'It doesn't matter,' said Joyce. 'I can take any kind of post now. My friend, whom I lived with, has – gone away.'

'Then you'd consider going abroad?'

Joyce nodded.

'Yes, as far away as possible.'

'Mr Allaby is here now, as it happens, interviewing candidates. I'll send you in to him.'

In another minute Joyce was sitting in a cubicle answering questions. Something about her interlocutor seemed vaguely familiar to her, but she could not place him. And then suddenly her mind awoke a little, aware that the last question was faintly out of the ordinary.

'Do you get on well with old ladies?' Mr Allaby was asking.

Joyce smiled in spite of herself.

'I think so.'

'You see my aunt, who lives with me, is rather difficult. She is very fond of me and she is a great dear really, but I fancy that a young woman might find her rather difficult sometimes.'

'I think I'm patient and good-tempered,' said Joyce, 'and I have always got on with elderly people very well.'

'You would have to do certain things for my aunt and otherwise you would have the charge of my little boy, who is three. His mother died a year ago.'

'I see.'

There was a pause.

'Then if you think you would like the post, we will consider that settled. We travel out next week. I will let you know the exact date, and I expect you would like a small advance of salary to fit yourself out.'

'Thank you very much. That would be very kind of you.'

They had both risen. Suddenly Mr Allaby said awkwardly:

'I – hate to butt in – I mean I wish – I would like to know – I mean, is your dog all right?'

For the first time Joyce looked at him. The colour

came into her face, her blue eyes deepened almost to black. She looked straight at him. She had thought him elderly, but he was not so very old. Hair turning grey, a pleasant weatherbeaten face, rather stooping shoulders, eyes that were brown and something of the shy kindliness of a dog's. He looked a little like a dog, Joyce thought.

'Oh, it's *you*,' she said. 'I thought afterwards – I never thanked you.'

'No need. Didn't expect it. Knew what you were feeling like. What about the poor old chap?'

The tears came into Joyce's eyes. They streamed down her cheeks. Nothing on earth could have kept them back.

'He's dead.'

'Oh!'

He said nothing else, but to Joyce that Oh! was one of the most comforting things she had ever heard. There was everything in it that couldn't be put into words.

After a minute or two he said jerkily:

'Matter of fact, I had a dog. Died two years ago. Was with a crowd of people at the time who couldn't understand making heavy weather about it. Pretty rotten to have to carry on as though nothing had happened.'

Joyce nodded.

'I *know* –' said Mr Allaby.

He took her hand, squeezed it hard and dropped it. He went out of the little cubicle. Joyce followed in a minute or two and fixed up various details with the ladylike person. When she arrived home. Mrs Barnes met her on the doorstep with that relish in gloom typical of her class.

'They've sent the poor little doggie's body home,' she announced. 'It's up in your room. I was saying to Barnes, and he's ready to dig a nice little hole in the back garden –'

Magnolia Blossom

I

Vincent Easton was waiting under the clock at Victoria Station. Now and then he glanced up at it uneasily. He thought to himself: 'How many other men have waited here for a woman who didn't come?'

A sharp pang shot through him. Supposing that Theo didn't come, that she had changed her mind? Women did that sort of thing. Was he sure of her – had he ever been sure of her? Did he really know anything at all about her? Hadn't she puzzled him from the first? There had seemed to be two women – the lovely, laughing creature who was Richard Darrell's wife, and the other – silent, mysterious, who had walked by his side in the garden of Haymer's Close. Like a magnolia flower – that was how he thought of her – perhaps because it was under the magnolia tree that they had tasted their first rapturous, incredulous kiss. The air had been sweet with the scent of magnolia bloom, and one or two petals, velvety-soft and fragrant, had floated down, resting on that upturned face that was as creamy and as soft and as silent as they. Magnolia blossom – exotic, fragrant, mysterious.

That had been a fortnight ago – the second day he had met her. And now he was waiting for her to come to him forever. Again incredulity shot through him. She wouldn't come. How could he ever have believed it? It would be giving up so much. The beautiful Mrs Darrell couldn't do this sort of thing quietly. It was bound to be a nine days' wonder, a far-reaching scandal that would never quite be forgotten. There were better, more expedient ways of doing these things – a discreet divorce, for instance.

But they had never thought of that for a moment – at least he had not. Had she, he wondered? He had never known anything of her thoughts. He had asked her to come away with him almost timorously – for after all, what was he? Nobody in particular – one of a thousand orange growers in the Transvaal. What a life to take her to – after the brilliance of London! And yet, since he wanted her so desperately, he must needs ask.

She had consented very quietly, with no hesitations or protests, as though it were the simplest thing in the world that he was asking her.

'Tomorrow?' he had said, amazed, almost unbelieving.

And she had promised in that soft, broken voice that was so different from the laughing brilliance of her social manner. He had compared her to a diamond when he first saw her – a thing of flashing fire, reflecting light from a hundred facets. But at that first touch, that first kiss, she had changed miraculously to the clouded softness of a pearl – a pearl like a magnolia blossom, creamy-pink.

She had promised. And now he was waiting for her to fulfil that promise.

He looked again at the clock. If she did not come soon, they would miss the train.

Sharply a wave of reaction set in. She wouldn't come! Of course she wouldn't come. Fool that he had been ever to expect it! What were promises? He would find a letter when he got back to his rooms – explaining, protesting, saying all the things that women do when they are excusing themselves for lack of courage.

He felt anger – anger and the bitterness of frustration.

Then he saw her coming towards him down the platform, a faint smile on her face. She walked slowly, without haste or fluster, as one who had all eternity before her. She was in black – soft black that clung, with a little black hat that framed the wonderful creamy pallor of her face.

He found himself grasping her hand, muttering stupidly:

'So you've come – you have come. After all!'

'Of course.'

How calm her voice sounded! How calm!

'I thought you wouldn't,' he said, releasing her hand and breathing hard.

Her eyes opened – wide, beautiful eyes. There was wonder in them, the simple wonder of a child.

'Why?'

He didn't answer. Instead he turned aside and requisitioned a passing porter. They had not much time. The next few minutes were all bustle and confusion. Then they were sitting in their reserved compartment and the drab houses of southern London were drifting by them.

II

Theodora Darrell was sitting opposite him. At last she was his. And he knew now how incredulous, up to the very last minute, he had been. He had not dared to let himself believe. That magical, elusive quality about her had frightened him. It had seemed impossible that she should ever belong to him.

Now the suspense was over. The irrevocable step

was taken. He looked across at her. She lay back in the corner, quite still. The faint smile lingered on her lips, her eyes were cast down, the long, black lashes swept the creamy curve of her cheek.

He thought: 'What's in her mind now? What is she thinking of? Me? Her husband? What does she think about him anyway? Did she care for him once? Or did she never care? Does she hate him, or is she indifferent to him?' And with a pang the thought swept through him: 'I don't know. I never shall know. I love her, and I don't know anything about her – what she thinks or what she feels.'

His mind circled round the thought of Theodora Darrell's husband. He had known plenty of married women who were only too ready to talk about their husbands – of how they were misunderstood by them, of how their finer feelings were ignored. Vincent Easton reflected cynically that it was one of the best-known opening gambits.

But except casually, Theo had never spoken of Richard Darrell. Easton knew of him what everybody knew. He was a popular man, handsome, with an engaging, carefree manner. Everybody liked Darrell. His wife always seemed on excellent terms with him. But that proved nothing, Vincent reflected. Theo was well-bred – she would not air her grievances in public.

And between them, no word had passed. From that

second evening of their meeting, when they had walked together in the garden, silent, their shoulders touching, and he had felt the faint tremor that shook her at his touch, there had been no explainings, no defining of the position. She had returned his kisses, a dumb, trembling creature, shorn of all that hard brilliance which, together with her cream-and-rose beauty, had made her famous. Never once had she spoken of her husband. Vincent had been thankful for that at the time. He had been glad to be spared the arguments of a woman who wished to assure herself and her lover that they were justified in yielding to their love.

Yet now the tacit conspiracy of silence worried him. He had again that panic-stricken sense of knowing nothing about this strange creature who was willingly linking her life to his. He was afraid.

In the impulse to reassure himself, he bent forward and laid a hand on the black-clad knee opposite him. He felt once again the faint tremor that shook her, and he reached up for her hand. Bending forward, he kissed the palm, a long, lingering kiss. He felt the response of her fingers on his and, looking up, met her eyes, and was content.

He leaned back in his seat. For the moment, he wanted no more. They were together. She was his. And presently he said in a light, almost bantering tone:

'You're very silent?'

'Am I?'

'Yes.' He waited a minute, then said in a graver tone: 'You're sure you don't – regret?'

Her eyes opened wide at that. 'Oh, no!'

He did not doubt the reply. There was an assurance of sincerity behind it.

'What are you thinking about? I want to know.'

In a low voice she answered: 'I think I'm afraid.'

'Afraid?'

'Of happiness.'

He moved over beside her then, held her to him and kissed the softness of her face and neck.

'I love you,' he said. 'I love you – love you.'

Her answer was in the clinging of her body, the abandon of her lips.

Then he moved back to his own corner. He picked up a magazine and so did she. Every now and then, over the top of the magazines, their eyes met. Then they smiled.

They arrived at Dover just after five. They were to spend the night there, and cross to the Continent on the following day. Theo entered their sitting room in the hotel with Vincent close behind her. He had a couple of evening papers in his hand which he threw down on the table. Two of the hotel servants brought in the luggage and withdrew.

Theo turned from the window where she had been

standing looking out. In another minute they were in each other's arms.

There was a discreet tap on the door and they drew apart again.

'Damn it all,' said Vincent, 'it doesn't seem as though we were ever going to be alone.'

Theo smiled. 'It doesn't look like it,' she said softly. Sitting down on the sofa, she picked up one of the papers.

The knock proved to be a waiter bearing tea. He laid it on the table, drawing the latter up to the sofa on which Theo was sitting, cast a deft glance round, inquired if there were anything further, and withdrew.

Vincent, who had gone into the adjoining room, came back into the sitting room.

'Now for tea,' he said cheerily, but stopped suddenly in the middle of the room. 'Anything wrong?' he asked.

Theo was sitting bolt upright on the sofa. She was staring in front of her with dazed eyes, and her face had gone deathly white.

Vincent took a quick step towards her.

'What is it, sweetheart?'

For answer she held out the paper to him, her finger pointing to the headline.

Vincent took the paper from her. 'FAILURE OF HOBSON, JEKYLL AND LUCAS,' he read. The name of the big city firm conveyed nothing to him at the moment, though he had an irritating conviction in the back of his mind that it ought to do so. He looked inquiringly at Theo.

'Richard is Hobson, Jekyll and Lucas,' she explained.

'Your husband?'

'Yes.'

Vincent returned to the paper and read the bald information it conveyed carefully. Phrases such as 'sudden crash', 'serious revelations to follow', 'other houses affected' struck him disagreeably.

Roused by a movement, he looked up. Theo was adjusting her little black hat in front of the mirror. She turned at the movement he made. Her eyes looked steadily into his.

'Vincent – I must go to Richard.'

He sprang up.

'Theo – don't be absurd.'

She repeated mechanically:

'I must go to Richard.'

'But, my dear –'

She made a gesture towards the paper on the floor.

'That means ruin – bankruptcy. I can't choose this day of all others to leave him.'

'You had left him before you heard of this. Be reasonable!'

She shook her head mournfully.

'You don't understand. I must go to Richard.'

And from that he could not move her. Strange that a creature so soft, so pliant, could be so unyielding. After the first, she did not argue. She let him say what he had to say unhindered. He held her in his arms, seeking to break her will by enslaving her senses, but though her soft mouth returned his kisses, he felt in her something aloof and invincible that withstood all his pleadings.

He let her go at last, sick and weary of the vain endeavour. From pleading he had turned to bitterness, reproaching her with never having loved him. That, too, she took in silence, without protest, her face, dumb and pitiful, giving the lie to his words. Rage mastered him in the end; he hurled at her every cruel word he could think of, seeking only to bruise and batter her to her knees.

At last the words gave out; there was nothing more to say. He sat, his head in his hands, staring down at the red pile carpet. By the door, Theodora stood, a black shadow with a white face.

It was all over.

She said quietly: 'Goodbye, Vincent.'

He did not answer.

The door opened – and shut again.

III

The Darrells lived in a house in Chelsea – an intriguing, old-world house, standing in a little garden of its own. Up the front of the house grew a magnolia tree, smutty, dirty, begrimed, but still a magnolia.

Theo looked up at it, as she stood on the doorstep some three hours later. A sudden smile twisted her mouth in pain.

She went straight to the study at the back of the house. A man was pacing up and down in the room – a young man, with a handsome face and a haggard expression.

He gave an ejaculation of relief as she came in.

'Thank God you've turned up, Theo. They said you'd taken your luggage with you and gone off out of town somewhere.'

'I heard the news and came back.'

Richard Darrell put an arm about her and drew her to the couch. They sat down upon it side by side. Theo drew herself free of the encircling arm in what seemed a perfectly natural manner.

'How bad is it, Richard?' she asked quietly.

'Just as bad as it can be – and that's saying a lot.'

'Tell me!'

He began to walk up and down again as he talked.

Theo sat and watched him. He was not to know that every now and then the room went dim, and his voice faded from her hearing, while another room in a hotel at Dover came clearly before her eyes.

Nevertheless she managed to listen intelligently enough. He came back and sat down on the couch by her.

'Fortunately,' he ended, 'they can't touch your marriage settlement. The house is yours also.'

Theo nodded thoughtfully.

'We shall have that at any rate,' she said. 'Then things will not be too bad? It means a fresh start, that is all.'

'Oh! Quite so. Yes.'

But his voice did not ring true, and Theo thought suddenly: 'There's something else. He hasn't told me everything.'

'There's nothing more, Richard?' she said gently. 'Nothing worse?'

He hesitated for just half a second, then: 'Worse? What should there be?'

'I don't know,' said Theo.

'It'll be all right,' said Richard, speaking more as though to reassure himself than Theo. 'Of course, it'll be all right.'

He flung an arm about her suddenly.

'I'm glad you're here,' he said. 'It'll be all right now

that you're here. Whatever else happens, I've got you, haven't I?'

She said gently: 'Yes, you've got me.' And this time she left his arm round her.

He kissed her and held her close to him, as though in some strange way he derived comfort from her nearness.

'I've got you, Theo,' he said again presently, and she answered as before: 'Yes, Richard.'

He slipped from the couch to the floor at her feet.

'I'm tired out,' he said fretfully. 'My God, it's been a day. Awful! I don't know what I should do if you weren't here. After all, one's wife is one's wife, isn't she?'

She did not speak, only bowed her head in assent.

He laid his head on her lap. The sigh he gave was like that of a tired child.

Theo thought again: 'There's something he hasn't told me. What is it?'

Mechanically her hand dropped to his smooth, dark head, and she stroked it gently, as a mother might comfort a child.

Richard murmured vaguely:

'It'll be all right now you're here. You won't let me down.'

His breathing grew slow and even. He slept. Her hand still smoothed his head.

But her eyes looked steadily into the darkness in front of her, seeing nothing.

'Don't you think, Richard,' said Theodora, 'that you'd better tell me everything?'

It was three days later. They were in the drawing room before dinner.

Richard started, and flushed.

'I don't know what you mean,' he parried.

'Don't you?'

He shot a quick glance at her.

'Of course there are – well – details.'

'I ought to know everything, don't you think, if I am to help?'

He looked at her strangely.

'What makes you think I want you to help?'

She was a little astonished.

'My dear Richard, I'm your wife.'

He smiled suddenly, the old, attractive, carefree smile.

'So you are, Theo. And a very good-looking wife, too. I never could stand ugly women.'

He began walking up and down the room, as was his custom when something was worrying him.

'I won't deny you're right in a way,' he said presently. 'There is something.'

He broke off.

'Yes?'

'It's so damned hard to explain things of this kind to women. They get hold of the wrong end of the stick – fancy a thing is – well, what it isn't.'

Theo said nothing.

'You see,' went on Richard, 'the law's one thing, and right and wrong are quite another. I may do a thing that's perfectly right and honest, but the law wouldn't take the same view of it. Nine times out of ten, everything pans out all right, and the tenth time you – well, hit a snag.'

Theo began to understand. She thought to herself: 'Why am I not surprised? Did I always know, deep down, that he wasn't straight?'

Richard went on talking. He explained himself at unnecessary lengths. Theo was content for him to cloak the actual details of the affair in this mantle of verbosity. The matter concerned a large tract of South African property. Exactly what Richard had done, she was not concerned to know. Morally, he assured her, everything was fair and above board; legally – well, there it was; no getting away from the fact, he had rendered himself liable to criminal prosecution.

He kept shooting quick glances at his wife as he talked. He was nervous and uncomfortable. And still he excused himself and tried to explain away that which a child might have seen in its naked truth. Then finally in a burst of justification, he broke down. Perhaps Theo's eyes, momentarily scornful, had something to do with it. He sank down in a chair by the fireplace, his head in his hands.

'There it is, Theo,' he said brokenly, 'What are you going to do about it?'

She came over to him with scarcely a moment's pause and, kneeling down by the chair, put her face against his.

'What can be done, Richard? What can we do?'

He caught her to him.

'You mean it? You'll stick to me?'

'Of course. My dear, of course.'

He said, moved to sincerity in spite of himself: 'I'm a thief, Theo. That's what it means, shorn of fine language – just a thief.'

'Then I'm a thief's wife, Richard. We'll sink or swim together.'

They were silent for a little while. Presently Richard recovered something of his jaunty manner.

'You know, Theo, I've got a plan, but we'll talk of that later. It's just on dinnertime. We must go and change. Put on that creamy thingummybob of yours, you know – the Caillot model.'

Theo raised her eyebrows quizzically.

'For an evening at home?'

'Yes, yes, I know. But I like it. Put it on, there's

a good girl. It cheers me up to see you looking your best.'

Theo came down to dinner in the Caillot. It was a creation in creamy brocade, with a faint pattern of gold running through it and an undernote of pale pink to give warmth to the cream. It was cut daringly low in the back, and nothing could have been better designed to show off the dazzling whiteness of Theo's neck and shoulders. She was truly now a magnolia flower.

Richard's eye rested upon her in warm approval. 'Good girl. You know, you look simply stunning in that dress.'

They went in to dinner. Throughout the evening Richard was nervous and unlike himself, joking and laughing about nothing at all, as if in a vain attempt to shake off his cares. Several times Theo tried to lead him back to the subject they had been discussing before, but he edged away from it.

Then suddenly, as she rose to go to bed, he came to the point.

'No, don't go yet. I've got something to say. You know, about this miserable business.'

She sat down again.

He began talking rapidly. With a bit of luck, the whole thing could be hushed up. He had covered his tracks fairly well. So long as certain papers didn't get into the receiver's hands –

He stopped significantly.

'Papers?' asked Theo perplexedly. 'You mean you will destroy them?'

Richard made a grimace.

'I'd destroy them fast enough if I could get hold of them. That's the devil of it all!'

'Who has them, then?'

'A man we both know – Vincent Easton.'

A very faint exclamation escaped Theo. She forced it back, but Richard had noticed it.

'I've suspected he knew something of the business all along. That's why I've asked him here a good bit. You may remember that I asked you to be nice to him?'

'I remember,' said Theo.

'Somehow I never seem to have got on really friendly terms with him. Don't know why. But he likes you. I should say he likes you a good deal.'

Theo said in a very clear voice: 'He does.'

'Ah!' said Richard appreciatively. 'That's good. Now you see what I'm driving at. I'm convinced that if you went to Vincent Easton and asked him to give you those papers, he wouldn't refuse. Pretty woman, you know – all that sort of thing.'

'I can't do that,' said Theo quickly.

'Nonsense.'

'It's out of the question.'

The red came slowly out in blotches on Richard's face. She saw that he was angry.

'My dear girl, I don't think you quite realize the position. If this comes out, I'm liable to go to prison. It's ruin – disgrace.'

'Vincent Easton will not use those papers against you. I am sure of that.'

'That's not quite the point. He mayn't realize that they incriminate me. It's only taken in conjunction with – with my affairs – with the figures they're bound to find. Oh! I can't go into details. He'll ruin me without knowing what he's doing unless somebody puts the position before him.'

'You can do that yourself, surely. Write to him.'

'A fat lot of good that would be! No, Theo, we've only got one hope. You're the trump card. You're my wife. You must help me. Go to Easton tonight –'

A cry broke from Theo.

'Not tonight. Tomorrow perhaps.'

'My God, Theo, can't you realize things? Tomorrow may be too late. If you could go now – at once – to Easton's rooms.' He saw her flinch, and tried to reassure her. 'I know, my dear girl, I know. It's a beastly thing to do. But it's life or death. Theo, you won't fail me? You said you'd do anything to help me –'

Theo heard herself speaking in a hard, dry voice. 'Not this thing. There are reasons.'

'It's life or death, Theo. I mean it. See here.'

He snapped open a drawer of the desk and took out a revolver. If there was something theatrical about that action, it escaped her notice.

'It's that or shooting myself. I can't face the racket. If you won't do as I ask you, I'll be a dead man before morning. I swear to you solemnly that that's the truth.'

Theo gave a low cry. 'No, Richard, not that!'

'Then help me.'

He flung the revolver down on the table and knelt by her side. 'Theo my darling – if you love me – if you've ever loved me – do this for me. You're my wife, Theo, I've no one else to turn to.'

On and on his voice went, murmuring, pleading. And at last Theo heard her own voice saying: 'Very well – yes.'

Richard took her to the door and put her into a taxi.

IV

'Theo!'

Vincent Easton sprang up in incredulous delight. She stood in the doorway. Her wrap of white ermine was hanging from her shoulders. Never, Easton thought, had she looked so beautiful.

'You've come after all.'

She put out a hand to stop him as he came towards her.

'No, Vincent, this isn't what you think.'

She spoke in a low, hurried voice.

'I'm here from my husband. He thinks there are some papers which may – do him harm. I have come to ask you to give them to me.'

Vincent stood very still, looking at her. Then he gave a short laugh.

'So that's it, is it? I thought Hobson, Jekyll and Lucas sounded familiar the other day, but I couldn't place them at the minute. Didn't know your husband was connected with the firm. Things have been going wrong there for some time. I was commissioned to look into the matter. I suspected some underling. Never thought of the man at the top.'

Theo said nothing. Vincent looked at her curiously.

'It makes no difference to you, this?' he asked. 'That – well, to put it plainly, that your husband's a swindler?'

She shook her head.

'It beats me,' said Vincent. Then he added quietly: 'Will you wait a minute or two? I will get the papers.'

Theo sat down in a chair. He went into the other room. Presently he returned and delivered a small package into her hand.

'Thank you,' said Theo. 'Have you a match?'

Taking the matchbox he proffered, she knelt down by the fireplace. When the papers were reduced to a pile of ashes, she stood up.

'Thank you,' she said again.

'Not at all,' he answered formally. 'Let me get you a taxi.'

He put her into it, saw her drive away. A strange, formal little interview. After the first, they had not even dared look at each other. Well, that was that, the end. He would go away, abroad, try and forget.

Theo leaned her head out of the window and spoke to the taxi driver. She could not go back at once to the house in Chelsea. She must have a breathing space. Seeing Vincent again had shaken her horribly. If only – if only. But she pulled herself up. Love for her husband she had none – but she owed him loyalty. He was down, she must stick by him. Whatever else he might have done, he loved her; his offence had been committed against society, not against her.

The taxi meandered on through the wide streets of Hampstead. They came out on the heath, and a breath of cool, invigorating air fanned Theo's cheeks. She had herself in hand again now. The taxi sped back towards Chelsea.

Richard came out to meet her in the hall.

'Well,' he demanded, 'you've been a long time.'

'Have I?'

'Yes – a very long time. Is it – all right?'

He followed her, a cunning look in his eyes. His hands were shaking.

'It's – it's all right, eh?' he said again.

'I burnt them myself.'

'Oh!'

She went on into the study, sinking into a big armchair. Her face was dead white and her whole body drooped with fatigue. She thought to herself: 'If only I could go to sleep now and never, never wake up again!'

Richard was watching her. His glance, shy, furtive, kept coming and going. She noticed nothing. She was beyond noticing.

'It went off quite all right, eh?'

'I've told you so.'

'You're sure they were the right papers? Did you look?'

'No.'

'But then –'

'I'm sure, I tell you. Don't bother me, Richard. I can't bear any more tonight.'

Richard shifted nervously.

'No, no. I see.'

He fidgeted about the room. Presently he came over to her, laid a hand on her shoulder. She shook it off.

'Don't touch me.' She tried to laugh. 'I'm sorry, Richard. My nerves are on edge. I feel I can't bear to be touched.'

'I know. I understand.'

Again he wandered up and down.

'Theo,' he burst out suddenly. 'I'm damned sorry.'

'What?' She looked up, vaguely startled.

'I oughtn't to have let you go there at this time of night. I never dreamed that you'd be subjected to any – unpleasantness.'

'Unpleasantness?' She laughed. The word seemed to amuse her. 'You don't know! Oh, Richard, you don't know!'

'I don't know what?'

She said very gravely, looking straight in front of her: 'What this night has cost me.'

'My God! Theo! I never meant – You – you did that, for me? The swine! Theo – Theo – I couldn't have known. I couldn't have guessed. My God!'

He was kneeling by her now stammering, his arms round her, and she turned and looked at him with faint surprise, as though his words had at last really penetrated to her attention.

'I – I never meant –'

'You never meant what, Richard?'

Her voice startled him.

'Tell me. What was it that you never meant?'

'Theo, don't let us speak of it. I don't want to know. I want never to think of it.'

She was staring at him, wide awake now, with every faculty alert. Her words came clear and distinct:

'You never meant – What do you think happened?'

'It didn't happen, Theo. Let's say it didn't happen.'

And still she stared, till the truth began to come to her.

'You think that –'

'I don't want –'

She interrupted him: 'You think that Vincent Easton asked a price for those letters? You think that I – paid him?'

Richard said weakly and unconvincingly: 'I – I never dreamed he was that kind of man.'

V

'Didn't you?' She looked at him searchingly. His eyes fell before hers. 'Why did you ask me to put on this dress this evening? Why did you send me there alone at this time of night? You guessed he – cared for me. You wanted to save your skin – save it at any cost – even at the cost of my honour.' She got up.

'I see now. You meant that from the beginning – or at least you saw it as a possibility, and it didn't deter you.'

'Theo –'

'You can't deny it. Richard, I thought I knew all there was to know about you years ago. I've known almost from the first that you weren't straight as regards the world. But I thought you were straight with me.'

'Theo –'

'Can you deny what I've just been saying?'

He was silent, in spite of himself.

'Listen, Richard. There is something I must tell you. Three days ago when this blow fell on you, the servants told you I was away – gone to the country. That was only partly true. I had gone away with Vincent Easton –'

Richard made an inarticulate sound. She held out a hand to stop him.

'Wait. We were at Dover. I saw a paper – I realized what had happened. Then, as you know, I came back.'

She paused.

Richard caught her by the wrist. His eyes burnt into hers.

'You came back – in time?'

Theo gave a short, bitter laugh.

'Yes, I came back, as you say, "in time", Richard.'

Her husband relinquished his hold on her arm. He stood by the mantelpiece, his head thrown back. He looked handsome and rather noble.

'In that case,' he said, 'I can forgive.'

'I cannot.'

The two words came crisply. They had the semblance and the effect of a bomb in the quiet room. Richard started forward, staring, his jaw dropped with an almost ludicrous effect.

'You – er – what did you say, Theo?'

'I said I cannot forgive! In leaving you for another man. I sinned – not technically, perhaps, but in intention, which is the same thing. But if I sinned, I sinned through love. You, too, have not been faithful to me since our marriage. Oh, yes, I know. That I forgave, because I really believed in your love for me. But the thing you have done tonight is different. It is an ugly thing, Richard – a thing no woman should forgive. You sold me, your own wife, to purchase safety!'

She picked up her wrap and turned towards the door.

'Theo,' he stammered out, 'where are you going?'

She looked back over her shoulder at him.

'We all have to pay in this life, Richard. For my sin I must pay in loneliness. For yours – well, you gambled with the thing you love, and you have lost it!'

'You are going?'

She drew a long breath.

'To freedom. There is nothing to bind me here.'

He heard the door shut. Ages passed, or was it a few, minutes? Something fluttered down outside the window – the last of the magnolia petals, soft, fragrant.